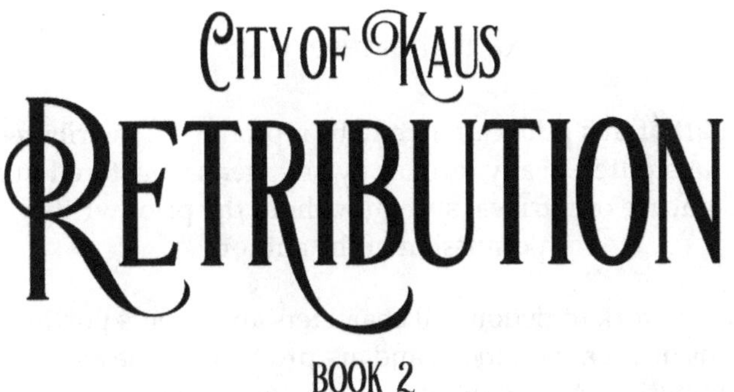

# City of Kaus
# RETRIBUTION

## BOOK 2

FoxTales Press

# DANI HOOTS

**Retribution**
**City of Kaus, #2**
First Edition © 2022 FoxTales Press
Edits by Victory Editing
Cover Art Copyright © 2021 Mona Finden
Cover Format Copyright © 2021 by Biserka
Designs



ISBN for Paperback: 978-1-956495-06-5
ISBN for Hardcover: 978-1-956495-05-8

*"Sometimes life is like this dark tunnel, you can't always see the light at the end of the tunnel, but if you just keep moving, you will come to a better place."*

—Uncle Iroh

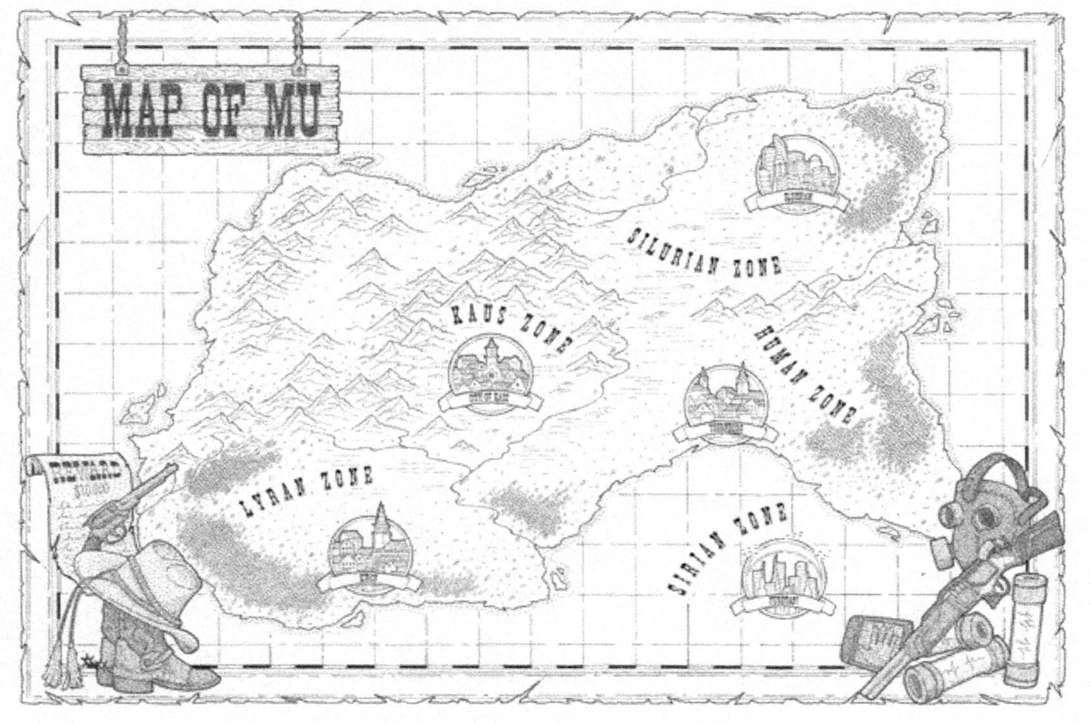

MAP OF MU
SILURIAN ZONE
HUMAN ZONE
KAUS ZONE
LYRAN ZONE
SIRIAN ZONE
REWARD

# CHAPTER I

Gabe

I didn't want to be doing this.

But it was the only place we would be safe, or at least that was what I had hoped. Since Byron, who was also my uncle, had made a huge plan to set up the Silurians on Zynon, I doubted he would have time to come find us, at least not right away. He had made Zach appear to be one of the Silurian leaders and then ordered the Silurians to open fire on all the people during the poker tournament. Many died, and we barely escaped with our lives. Luckily Byron had lost sight of all of us, and we fled before it was too late.

Now we were heading down to the Sirian Zone where I was from. Well, not only from but was the son of the queen. I supposed I was a prince, not that anyone down there cared. I was half-human, so in their eyes, I wasn't really a Sirian. It made it easier to run away and never look back. But there I was—looking back and waiting for the shuttle to take us down to the ocean floor.

And then what? I didn't know what the next plan of action was. Byron had set up the Silurians for a war against the other nations. They made them appear to be traitors. It was only a matter of time before fighting would ensue and the Silurians would be like the Kausians—conspirators who no longer had a home to go to.

Having learned the truth—now knowing that my uncle was responsible—I felt sick. I knew the sins of my ancestors had nothing to do with me, but I couldn't help but feel guilty. I had to do something—I had to make this right.

Which was why I knew we needed to come here and convince the Sirians—convince my mother—that

Byron was the one behind it all and that he had to be stopped.

Problem was, no one except my mother liked me. They thought I was an abomination. It wasn't just in my head either, as they had said so, many times, growing up. That was why I ran away.

I stared out at the ocean—the ocean that made up the Sirian Nation. The two suns were setting on the horizon, making the sky a beautiful orange and pink that was reflected in the water. A few seagulls cawed in the distance, and the sweet, salty scent of the sea permeated the air. It was a smell I missed.

Below the deep waters was my home of Furutani. It was where my mother and all her relatives and friends and the citizens of the Sirian Zone resided. Well, most of them. Although Sirians left the oceans often, there were many more who did not. And few people of other races got to visit the city without some sort of reason, such as diplomatic meetings and the like. Which made bringing three Kausians with me problematic.

"Everything all right?" Cor stepped up beside me.

I turned to him and examined his familiar features. He had a perfectly chiseled jaw, hair as white as snow, and golden eyes that marked him as a Kausian. He was wearing some cheap clothing we had bought on the transport as we made our escape from Byron, as was I. I was used to seeing him in flawlessly tailored suits. I sort of liked the change.

I gave him my most convincing smile. "Yeah. Everything is just peachy."

He grabbed my hand and squeezed. "Know I'm here for you. I understand what it's like to run from one's past. I've got your back, okay?"

I leaned in and kissed him. His lips tasted like the chicken wings he had devoured on the ship that had brought us down from the moon Zynon. "Thank you."

We hadn't finished our talk about Ellie and where their relationship was in the mix. Too much had happened and too much was still happening. But once this all slowed down, I would have the courage to ask him for the truth—ask him if he wanted to be with me.

And I feared the answer was no.

We had been together for two years, so I thought our relationship was quite solid. But he never really told me he was once engaged, and that was what the wooden ring he always kept on his person was. The fact that he had hidden it from me for so long made me think he never lost his love for her. Which meant if she loved

"We'll be safest underwater. Byron won't be able to get there without us knowing, at least that's what I'm hoping. He has spies everywhere else, and he could sneak up on us. And we may be able to convince the council to help us."

"You don't think they'll realize the truth?" Cor asked.

"Do I think the half-Sirian and three Kausians will persuade people who look down on them that one of their favorite humans did wrong?"

"Fair enough. I guess we'll just have to be convincing."

"That we will. But for now, we just need to gather our thoughts and stay out of Byron's hair. My mother has a lot of rooms available, so we should be able to take a breather and think about what to do next."

Cor let go of my hand, and I turned to him. He bit his lip, as if thinking of something.

"What is it?" I asked.

"What if we didn't go? What if we didn't let all this weigh us down? Why don't we run away? Wait for everything to just… happen? I mean, we could find a nice cave or something and let the world pass us by."

I shook my head. "You can't stay still any more than I can. Besides, don't you want revenge on Byron?"

Cor slowly nodded. "Yeah, I do. But I don't think I realized how deep and dark this all went. I don't know if we'll be able to take him down at this rate. He's powerful and has people backing him up everywhere. It sounds like this has been something he and his father and grandfather have been planning for decades. Can we really do anything to stop it?"

I shrugged. "Isn't it worth a shot? I mean, I'm as afraid as you are. I know what he's capable of, Cor. Believe me when I say I'm terrified. I always have been. But would the world be worth living in if he succeeds?"

He rubbed his white hair, causing it to be messier than it already was. "Yeah, I suppose you're right. I just hate all this. It isn't fair."

"I agree. It isn't. But perhaps after all this is over, it will be a little more fair. Or it will be less fair, depending on who wins."

I heard footsteps behind us and turned to find Ellie and Zach. Ellie was back in pants, which made her happy. She hated all the nice dresses I had picked up for her. Her long, wavy dark hair was pulled back in a ponytail, and she had a resting bitch face that made anyone nearby stay clear of her. Zach, on the other hand, was a big cinnamon roll. They definitely contrasted not only in demeanor but also in the way they appeared. Zach had bright copper-colored hair and pale skin, which was due to him being half-human, half-Kausian. The only thing of his that was similar to the others was his golden eyes.

I gave them a smile. "Were you able to take care of your horses?"

Ellie nodded. "Yup. They should be good to go for two weeks. I figured overestimating was better than underestimating; otherwise, they might sell our horses."

Zach added, "It was hard to say goodbye to my dear Charlotte Hunkerbink III, but it's for the best. They wouldn't do well underwater."

Cor let out a short laugh. "You named your horse Charlotte Hunkerbink III?"

"Indeed I did. Why? What's wrong with that name?"

Cor shook his head. "Nothing. It's just definitely a name you would come up with." He turned to Ellie. "What about you? What did you name your dear horse?"

"Kevin," she answered.

Cor laughed even harder. "Perfect. Neither of those names surprise me."

Ellie smacked Cor on the arm as he kept laughing. I noticed a sliver of a smile on her lips. She obviously still had feelings for him. I took a long breath and let it out slowly. This was going to be one interesting trip.

# CHAPTER II

Ellie

Gabe didn't seem excited to be going home. I hadn't heard many details from Gabe himself, but by what Zach had said about Byron and the fact Byron was Gabe's uncle and had hired us to kill him, I could imagine. Gabe was half-Sirian, half-human, and if life was anything like it had been for Zach, it wasn't fun.

And the Sirians didn't like any other race to begin with. It must have been horrible growing up in the middle of it all, not to mention being the leader's own son. I would have hoped that being part of the royal family would have helped, but I supposed it could make other things worse. He probably dealt with comments and looks and couldn't ever hide since he was in the public eye constantly. It made sense he ran away and lied about who and what he was. Even to Cor.

It wasn't as if Cor didn't have his own secrets he kept hidden from everyone close to him.

I understood why Gabe thought it would be safe to go home to hide, as it was hard for any non-Sirian to get into the city. Even though Byron was sort of family, he would have to go through some paperwork. He could then order the people at the station, or border, to alert him when any human had set foot in the capital Furutani. At least, that was what we were hoping.

Besides going into the middle of the woods and wishing for the best, there was no place for us to hide from Byron on land. It was likely he had men everywhere in the Human and Lyran Zones. We needed time to think, and that wouldn't be possible if we had to look behind our backs constantly or figure out how to get out of a jail cell or whatnot. Although we had been doing that for three years now, I felt a bit more was at stake.

On top of simply hiding, we were also trying to convince the Sirians to help us defeat Byron and to persuade the other nations that he was a monster who wanted only the humans to exist. I had no idea how we were going to achieve that. Even if Gabe was her son, that didn't mean she would listen to everything her son said. She would see that he was hanging out with some Kausians and assume we were warping his mind or something. No nation saw us as anything but corrupt, sly, and pushing our own agenda for some quick cash. It was sickening to really know how other nations viewed us.

We would also have to convince her that not only did the father of her child's brother cause the destruction of Kaus but also that her son's great-grandfather was the one who started to warp everyone's thoughts about us. And how he was the one who began this treacherous plan. I mean, who wouldn't believe that?

I knew the odds were slim for her to believe us, but I had to hope. Hope was the only thing we had. If these people didn't cooperate with us—if we were all alone—I didn't know how we were going to take down Byron. He was smart, cunning, and had way too many people backing him up.

But on the other hand, we had nothing to lose. Our people were almost all destroyed, and if Byron won, then other nations would be wiped out as well. One would think the societies would team up or have some peace conference, but none of them got along enough to enter any kind of treaty. And by the time they'd realize what was happening, it will be too late.

Which was why we had to act fast.

We had nothing to gather as the underwater transport made it to the dock, as we left everything up on Zynon. All I had were the clothes we bought on the transport from the moon, my favorite gun, and the ring that Cor had given me all those years ago. As I followed the others boarding the ship, I touched my shirt where the ring lay beneath it.

I didn't know what to make of my feelings for Cor. I had hated him for so long, but I had loved him for much longer before that. My feelings were swirling, and I couldn't discern them from each other. He had lied to me but only because he wanted to make a good life for us. But he trusted the wrong person, and that man destroyed our kind.

So was Cor in the wrong? Or if he hadn't been the one who leaked the info, would it just have been someone else?

Cor was the only person besides his parents who knew the codes to the shield over Kaus. He was supposed to be training to take over, but he never told his parents he was getting secret lessons from some human in order to go to the university. That person was Byron, however, and he'd threatened Cor until he'd given him the codes. The Silurians then took those codes and destroyed our kind. Cor never could have imagined that was their plan, and I don't believe I could have either. I would have expected an invasion or takeover—not complete genocide.

So the feelings in my heart were completely scrambled. I was mad at him, and yet I understood. I wanted more than anything to go back to what we used to have, but we both had changed over the years. I'm a bounty hunter and had killed people, and he was a prostitute and bounty hunter. And he had a boyfriend.

But Cor still had the ring.

At least, that was what Gabe had told me. Did that mean Cor still had feelings for me? Knowing Cor, he probably didn't even know himself. With everything going on, none of us had time to get our feelings straight.

And I felt that we wouldn't have time for a while.

It was best to put it all aside and focus on the mission at hand. Then, when it was all over, if we were still alive, we could figure it all out. It would be easier if he didn't have someone else. Gabe was a great guy, and I didn't want to hurt him. But I also had to be true to my feelings as well.

We stepped onto the ship, and I glanced around. There were some spots leaking where the panels met each other, and I wondered how secure this transport really was. None of the workers or Sirian passengers seemed to pay it much mind, so I didn't worry about it. The metal was dark, and the air was damp and chilly. It reminded me of the few cells Zach and I had spent time residing in the more rural towns. Good times.

I hadn't seen an underwater ship in person before, as most of the time Sirians swam to their city since they could breathe underwater. It wasn't until they'd let in other races as visitors that they made transports, although most of these passengers were Sirians.

But I doubted Kausians were welcomed.

Cor had handed all of us some dark glasses, and Gabe was the one to talk to the check-in attendant. He flashed some sort of card he had in his wallet, and it didn't seem like the attendant was going to press him for any more information.

So he hadn't been lying—he was the son of the leader here.

It made sense he could get us in without them taking too much notice that we were wearing dark glasses in this dimly lit machine. A lot of fancy people wore things that weren't practical—especially humans, which was what we appeared like. It wouldn't be until we got there that people would notice something was up as most Sirians didn't wear glasses, and I would assume that was how it was in the capital. Then they would notice what we were. Then the prejudice would show.

After he sorted everything out, Gabe led us to a little private cabin. It was similar to a train cabin but with waterproof fabric on the chairs and the walls were all metallic except for the wall facing out. That wall was mainly glass and revealed the wondrous ocean. It was a deep blue, and the seawater was so clear that you could see miles below.

I took a seat closest to the window, then stepped up to the glass as a little blue fish stared in at us. It scurried away, not liking the attention. Zach sat next to me and pointed at one of the creatures.

"Look at that one! It looks derpy!"

It truly did. It was colorful with a large forehead, if it was its forehead. Its eyes were also huge, and its mouth was hanging open as if it didn't know what it was doing.

I pointed at a different one. "How about that one? It almost looks like a rainbow shimmering in the light." It swam around some more before scurrying off like the bluefish had. The derpy one hadn't moved much, however. It must not have gotten the memo.

He nodded. "Indeed it does."

Gabe and Cor took their seats across from us. Although I hadn't been quite used to their fancy attire, now they were in more common wear as we didn't have much option on the ship back from Zynon. I had a feeling that would be remedied the moment we got to the Sirian Zone. Gabe had been fidgeting with his cuffs for hours ever since they changed, always frowning. He was definitely a rich kid at heart.

Cor ruffled his white hair a little and gave me his cocky smile. "Remember when we went fishing and Zach accidentally hooked that Lyran in the leg?"

I laughed. "I do! We had never run so hard."

Zach shook his head as he turned away from the

ocean. "That wasn't funny, you two. I almost died that day."

"He wouldn't have killed you," Cor commented. "Believe me—I have pissed off enough Lyrans through the years. He would have just mauled you until you couldn't move."

"Oh, so much better."

I kept grinning at the memory. That summer was a lot of fun, as it was full of fishing and laughter and a few death threats. We used to get into the worst trouble, although that hadn't changed. Now, instead of simple accidents and typical things teenagers did, we were in trouble for bounty hunting and beating people at the gambling tables. They always claimed I cheated, but I never did.

"So," I began as I turned to Gabe. "What's your mom like?"

Gabe fidgeted with his coat, as if surprised by the question. It did come out of nowhere, I had to admit, but I wanted to get the full story before we got there. His dark eyes that matched his hair glanced around a bit, as if searching for the right answer.

"A typical mother, I suppose. She always has to know what I'm doing and has people consistently on the lookout for me, hence why you could find me. She is sweet and kind, which I feel people take advantage of quite frequently. She is the only one who loved me growing up but was blind to the fact that most people hated me. I'm not sure if it was because she could never come to terms with the fact that I was different or if she didn't notice."

Cor patted Gabe's leg. I felt a sting of jealousy as I wished I was as close to him still. Would that change after all this was over? Or would we go our separate ways?

It shouldn't hurt this much. I had been hating him for three years—I should be over him. But after learning the truth and seeing his face again, all those feelings were coming back. I knew I should move on, just like he was. All of that was in the past. I had to let go.

At least, that was what my mind said. My heart did not seem to agree. Why emotions and logic never seemed to be on the same side, I did not understand.

"What's her full name again? I never did get the hang of remembering all the leaders' names back in school," Zach said.

"Queen Lili Araseis II. Apparently my great-grandmother was also named Lili. I was given my father's last name, which didn't help with the problem of standing out."

I wanted to ask more about that when the ship moved, which deterred my attention from any thoughts other than needing to find a bucket to puke in. All three of us Kausians quickly reached for the one bucket in the room.

"I'll go see if I can find some more buckets." Gabe sighed as he got up to search the corridor.

# CHAPTER III

Cor

We were approaching the city.

Although I had seen the city at a distance before while swimming when I was a kid, I had never gotten this close to it. It was magnificent, to say the least. I caught sight of a whale moving closely to the spires of the building I assumed was the palace. It moved slowly, its tail appearing as if it were going to hit one of the windows. It didn't, of course, as it was more than likely used to swimming around here and the buildings could hold up to such forces. Although it was the tallest building, there were many other buildings that were also tall and protruded into the water. It seemed that the Sirians built up rather than out. I wondered if that saved on materials or if there was a different reason.

From what I knew of the city, all the buildings were connected with tunnels in the water, similar to the moon base we had just been on. Although Sirians could swim for long periods of time underwater, they did need air eventually, just like a whale or any other mammal. How they got air to cycle down here, I was not sure. It was probably also similar to the moon base on Zynon.

The buildings were made of mostly glass and some metal similar to the ship we were on. As I thought about being on a mode of transportation, I cradled the bucket Gabe had found for me. I hated modes of transportation —I always got so sick. It wasn't fair as other species never got this sick. I wondered what it could have been caused by. Perhaps it was because we were shape-shifters. All I knew for sure was I would enjoy the scenery far more once we were there.

I glanced over to Gabe, who was staring out the glass. He wasn't exactly frowning, but he wasn't smiling either. He appeared as if he were deep in thought, wondering what the next few hours would bring. We were all in the same boat for that thought as we needed to help defeat Byron. But going back to a place one was running away from was a whole different story. I had been back where Kaus used to stand a couple of times over the years. It wasn't easy, and both times weren't by choice. However, it was where I had met Gabe.

Placing my hand on his shoulder, I squeezed it. "Don't worry. I'm here for you."

As I said those words, I felt like it was a lie. Would I always be there for him or only when it was easier? Or only when I was getting something out of it? Throughout our relationship, we had simply been using each other. I needed him to get close to Krax, and he was using me because he needed someone to keep him safe. Now we knew the truth about each other—now I knew he was a prince.

Although I had my own secrets, I didn't know how I felt about his lying about something so huge. I would have gone about all this in a different way. And I would have understood why people were after him.

And perhaps I would have used him as leverage…

I shook my head. No, I wouldn't have done that. I

turned my attention to Zach and Ellie, who had managed to fall asleep. Ellie's head was leaning on Zach's shoulder. They had always been close, even when we were all kids, but seeing how close they were now—realizing I had missed out on a lot—ate at me more than I wanted. I had Gabe. I had a new life that I quite enjoyed, other than needing to get revenge on what happened to my people. I had made the decision to not care about the future as I had doubted I would be alive when all this was over.

But that was when I thought the person who destroyed our people was Krax. Now that I knew it was the man who had gained my trust and betrayed me, things were different. Now that there were more people on my side.

Now that I'd seen her face again.

I took a deep breath and let it out slowly. I wouldn't get distracted. I had to fulfill my goal no matter the cost. I had to make this right. If not for myself, then for all the ghosts of our loved ones.

Kicking Ellie and Zach in the legs, I decided it was time for the snoozefest to end. "Rise and shine! We're almost there."

Ellie snorted as her head rose. I held back a laugh. It

was the most adorable thing ever, but I knew she would kill me if I said that. Zach yawned and stretched, almost smacking Ellie in the face with the back of his palm.

"Hey, watch it," Ellie commented as she dodged his arm.

Zach smiled. "What? You don't want to be whacked first thing in the morning? Or night? I'm not sure what time it is."

"It's still night I think," I said.

Gabe nodded. "It is on land, but down here it's morning. My mother will be expecting us to go straight to the palace. Then we can get a couple of hours of rest before deciding what to do next."

Ellie stretched her own arms—hitting Zach in the cheek on purpose. "That sounds like a good plan to me. Zach doesn't make the best pillow."

Zach frowned. "Hey, I like to think I make a great pillow."

I wanted to comment that she could use me for a pillow, but I knew that would be out of line for a couple of reasons. One of them was sitting next to me, and we still hadn't finished our conversation about Ellie. Second reason was I still wasn't sure how I felt about seeing her again. The plan was that I would either die before she found me or I would let her kill me. I knew she blamed me for everything that had happened, and I didn't mind dying if it was by her hands. She had every right to kill me—our people were gone thanks to me and my foolishness. I deserved to be killed for my sins.

However, after hearing what happened, it was almost as if she had forgiven me. She had hated me for years—did our love outweigh that hate? And would she be willing to take me back after everything?

The problem was, did I want to be taken back? I had Gabe now and we were happy, or at least I felt we were. I loved him, and it was a love that I could never compare to Ellie. It was different, but I didn't know which one was stronger. Gabe and I definitely had an open relationship, especially since I was a prostitute by trade, but it wasn't until I saw Ellie did I really understand that our openness was sexual in nature and had nothing to do with love.

I honestly didn't know what to do with this situation.

So I would focus on stopping Byron and not worrying about the other things that were right in front of me. They didn't matter right now even if my heart was aching and my brain wouldn't stop thinking about it.

I couldn't wait until this was all over and we all finally had a stable life, if that was even possible. Everything would fall into place. It had to. Karma owed us that much.

"Did you both sleep well?" I asked, trying to ignore my pressing thoughts, as if that were possible.

Ellie shrugged. "As well as normal. I have to admit, these seats are more comfortable than most of the beds we have stayed in over the years, even back in Kaus."

She had a point there. We were lucky if we even had a bed, let alone something as comfy as this. "Yeah, I suppose you are right."

"Don't worry." Gabe smiled. "You'll get to sleep in the most luscious beds in the Sirian Zone once we get to my mother's. She spares no expenses, especially when it comes to guests."

"As long as I get to share a bed with you, I don't care how comfy it is." I gave him a kiss on the cheek.

Gabe blushed as I noticed him glance at Ellie. Perhaps I shouldn't have made that comment, but it wasn't like it was news we were together. We had already been staying in the same bed since they had arrived in Zynon, not to mention they knew I was a prostitute. I had slept in many a bed over the past couple of years.

The ship shifted, and we three Kausians tried our best not to throw up again, but Zach didn't win that fight. He grabbed his bucket and threw up whatever was left in his stomach. Ellie patted his back.

"Don't worry. We'll be there soon. After this turn, we'll dock and you all won't have to worry about your motion sickness."

"Yeah," Zach commented. "Easy for you to say. We also will have to leave this place, which involves getting back on the ship."

"Unless we swim," Gabe commented. "It will be easier to do that leaving than arriving."

He had a point there. If we arrived and transformed, then they would have arrested us—but if we transform as we left and rise up somewhere where there weren't many people, then no one could throw us into prison. That is, if we were lucky. Sometimes it seemed like there was always someone in the wrong place at the wrong time. And we were the ones who paid for it.

Just as Ellie said, the ship stopped moving, and I felt a rush of fresh air come into the ship. Or, at least, it felt like fresh air. We were finally there. I followed Gabe as he stood up and left the private room we had. Ellie and

Zach followed suit.

As we made our way through the ship, I glanced out the glass at the buildings that made up the capital of the Sirian Zone. The spires went up high into the water, although even with how high they were, I couldn't quite see the surface of the sea. As for where the light outside came from, I had no idea. Some of it was coming from inside the buildings, but there seemed to be some on the outside coming from somewhere else.

"It's magnificent," Ellie whispered as she glanced around. "I mean, we have swum somewhat close to the city before, but I haven't ever been in the actual city."

"I definitely agree. I think it's far more beautiful than any other city, although I do like the human markets and such," Gabe commented.

I wondered how much he missed the Sirian capital or if he was just saying it to save face. I knew I missed Kaus, but a lot of it was clouded in pain. I tried not to think about it too much and wondered how much he thought about his home. He had never talked to me about it, then again, he never told me he was half Sirian, so I didn't know he was from here.

We stepped out of the ship, and Gabe nodded toward the palace. "Well, we should probably go to my mother's first. Shall we?"

# CHAPTER IV

Zach

Well if it weren't for all the stares, this would be one of the most magnificent places ever.

I felt the eyes go straight toward us the moment we stepped into the city. I didn't know if it was because they knew we weren't Sirians or if it was because they recognized Gabe. If he was their ruler's son, then it was highly possible that it was him they were staring at.

Gabe didn't seem to notice, or perhaps he didn't care as he was used to it all. I knew that feeling. In my own hometown, I was ostracized since I was also half-human. I didn't understand what it mattered to these people or anyone—we were still living, breathing, and had a will. We were all the same. We all deserved to be respected. Clearly, however, that wasn't the case.

And it was all because of Byron and his ancestors.

I still couldn't believe that Byron's grandfather had set this all up—had warped everyone into hating each other. I wondered what it was like a few generations before. There couldn't have been too much mingling, as there weren't many half-humans out there. But perhaps people still got along a bit better or simply kept to themselves. Probably the latter. But apparently the hatred toward Kausians wasn't as bad as it was before we were alive. How could only a hundred years make such a big difference? How could people change views so quickly? And could they all forget?

I supposed it all had to do with education and the like. If one could change history books, then they could tell people what did or didn't happen. They could completely make things up. It was scary to think such people had that much power.

A little kid holding a goldfish plushy stared at us while we walked by, his dark eyes as wide as they could be. His mouth was open a little, revealing his tiny sharp teeth, which I assumed would be replaced with larger sharp teeth when he was older like humans. His skin was dry and a bit scaly, as were most Sirians. Gabe definitely didn't appear as Sirian since he was half-human, which must have really made him stand out here. At least he could fit in with the humans, unlike me. I still had glowing yellow eyes which separated me from any other race, but my red hair stood out as no other Kausian had such a color. Gabe's eyes, although dark, weren't as dark as a normal Sirian's, and his teeth were like that of a human's. I wasn't sure if that was from cosmetic surgery or if he was born that way. His skin, although a little dry, wasn't the same. I wondered how much that would change if he was in the water—and whether his legs would turn into fins.

Not paying attention to all the staring and murmurs, Gabe led us through the city. Ellie, Cor, and I stayed close to him. We definitely didn't want to get lost here as I doubted anyone would help us or believe that we were guests to the ruler's son. They would probably arrest us or throw us out of the city.

We passed by shops that were similar to what one would see in the human or Lyran zone, but these shops were all in a lot better shape and weren't dusty since there wasn't any dust down here. There were shops for clothing and trinkets and glassware—all of which would be fun to explore.

Soon we came upon a row of restaurants. As I expected, they were all serving fish as I could smell the fumes coming from the kitchens. This caused my stomach to grumble. Hopefully we would eat soon as there was nothing left in my stomach now.

Glancing at Ellie, I found that she was staring at the back of Cor's head. I rolled my eyes. I knew she wasn't going to be able to go through with killing him like she thought she would, but I didn't think she would fall in love with him all over again. He had broken her heart, and yet that love for him still seemed to be there. Granted he was cunning and usually could make anyone around him feel special.

That's why that day was such a surprise. We would have never guessed that he would betray our kind— betray us—and let the Silurians in. I felt betrayed, as did Ellie.

But there was more to the story, just as always. He had been tricked or threatened. Either way, he hadn't done it willingly. I couldn't blame him, as Byron had used me to start a war with the Silurians. I could have said no. I could have sacrificed myself, but I didn't, and neither did Cor.

However, we had to blame someone. We had to direct our wrath somewhere. Now we knew the truth. Now we knew who was really behind it all.

And now we had to stop him from destroying all the other nations.

However, that didn't mean I forgave Cor for leaving us behind. He could have come to us—he could have told us the truth. Instead, he ran away, letting us pick up the pieces. Letting Ellie pick up the pieces. It took months for her to come to terms with what had happened. So for her to believe him so quickly and fall in love with him, I wondered if she simply wished for things to go back to normal. And I understood that feeling. I wanted things to go back to normal as well. But that wasn't going to happen. Nothing could go back to what it was.

Besides, he had a boyfriend now. Did Ellie think he was going to push Gabe aside for her? Did she think she could love him after he had seemed to move on? It ate at me that he could love someone after what he had done—if he truly loved Gabe. Perhaps he was just a diversion for his heart—a heart that was clearly corrupt.

I needed to stop thinking about it. The more I thought about it, the more hatred seemed to bubble up out of nowhere for Cor. Perhaps I couldn't forgive him—perhaps I wasn't as kind as people made me out to be. Either way, I needed a distraction.

I stepped up next to Ellie. "Do you think this really was a good idea? I don't know if we're really welcome here."

Ellie glanced around. "I don't think it will be as bad once we get into the palace. But honestly, nowhere else is better. We can't get into the Silurian Zone that easily, not to mention there is still a Silurian bounty on our heads. And it is more than likely closed off now. Then for the other zones, Byron probably has people everywhere looking for us. The Sirians, however, don't typically care about other nation's affairs. Even if the monarch's husband or whatever is human, Byron won't be able to step in here without some sort of paperwork —paperwork Gabe should be able to get his hands on."

"How do we know they won't betray us? I mean, for all we know, the monarchy and everyone in the palace could be wrapped around his finger like everyone else is," I pointed out.

Ellie shrugged. "I guess we'll just have to see. Gabe wants to try to convince his mother about all the stuff Byron has done and how we want to save the world. Unless Byron really has the queen wrapped around his finger, then we should be fine."

For some reason that didn't reassure me, but I tried not to think about it. There was only one way to know the future and that was by living it. One couldn't be too prepared though, especially in our line of work.

I glanced around at the built environment. It always baffled me that they were able to build all this underwater, but I supposed when you could stay underwater for long periods of time, it wouldn't be too difficult. They did need air after a while though, which was why they built this city. Then they didn't have to stay on Mu any longer. It wasn't like there were any other continents that were habitable, not to mention the storms far off in the water. Sailors were said to leave and never come back. After some time, people didn't try. No, instead they went to the moon because somehow that was easier.

People never made sense to me.

The Pleiadians, however, were able to find a place they could live on that was away from everyone. No one knew what the landscape there was as the Pleiadians would kill anyone who came near except for a couple of merchants. Surprisingly, Pleiadians made the best wine.

A cute little pufferfish swam by the glass, making me smile. I had yet to see one puff up in person and only saw them puffed up dried at markets. I thought about scaring it, but that didn't seem fair to the pufferfish. I would let it go on its merry way without fear.

There were a few Sirians swimming in the distance beyond the glass. I could see them from the glow of the city. I wasn't sure of the origin of the light. It didn't seem to be electricity but more like some kind of luminescence. The Sirians in the water all had spears, hunting for fish to sell or eat themselves. I wasn't much of a fish person, but I had a feeling down here I wouldn't have much of a choice when it came down to it. That was fine—at this point I would eat anything.

We arrived at the palace. I stared up at it in awe. There were guards not only stationed at the corridor leading to the entrance but also in the water beyond the glass, making sure there were no outside threats. I gulped as we came up to them. This would either go very smoothly or very poorly. If Ellie and my past experiences were consistent, there was going to be at least an argument, if not more.

Ellie and I stood behind Gabe and Cor as we approached the guards. Gabe swung his arms up.

"The great son of the queen is back. Please let us through."

The guards glanced at each other. "We weren't given any information about the prince of the Sirian Zone being back. How do we know it's you? The prince has been gone for a couple of years now."

Gabe let out a sigh. "Really? You two can't remember what I look like?"

They shook their heads. "We never met the son, and we wouldn't believe him to come to us with a group of..." The guard glanced at us and immediately appeared flustered. "Kausians? Not to mention you are wearing rags."

So I was right—there was going to be difficulty. It could never be easy for us, could it?

Gabe pulled out a card. "Is this good enough for you?"

I presumed it was some ID card that proved his royalty. He must have had it on him constantly as we didn't have time to go back to our room and grab anything. It wasn't like I had any possessions that I cared for, and Ellie had the one thing she cared for on her constantly. As did Cor, apparently.

One guard scanned the ID with some contraption I hadn't seen before—or at least never had to use before. After a moment, the man's eyes widened. He bowed and the other guard followed suit.

"We're so sorry. Will you please forgive our rudeness? We simply didn't realize you would be coming back."

Gabe smiled. "It is all right. Please alert my mother that I'm here and I'll be meeting her in the throne room."

They both nodded and one took off to alert the queen ahead of us.

Gabe turned to us. "Well then, shall we go see my mother?"

# CHAPTER V

Gabe

I tried not to act it, but I was nervous—more nervous than I had been in the gambling area when Byron wanted to kill me. Well, maybe not quite that nervous. But my heart was definitely pounding in my chest right now and I was sweating, which I didn't even think was possible for Sirians. Apparently since I was half-human, I could still sweat a little when I was super nervous.

Now I knew.

It was mostly my hands that were clammy. I wiped

them nonchalantly on my clothes as I tried to keep the facade of belonging here. I didn't—I never did. I was an outcast the moment I was born. I didn't expect the guards to let me in without consulting my mother first. But they must have been new, and no one talked about me anymore.

I didn't know if that was better or worse.

I had seemed to be forgotten—as if they all could move on since the disgusting half-human was gone. I didn't mean anything to these people. It wasn't as if I would ever have a chance to rule. No, that honor would go to a different person. That would go to my little sister.

A couple of years before I ran away, my mother had a child with a Sirian diplomat. She knew there would be no way the people would let me lead. No, there would be a rebellion. So she had another kid—my baby sister Kishiko, named after our great-grandmother. She also took the last name Araseis, whereas I took my father's last name, Pickett. That did not help with my standing out.

I didn't get to spend much time with my sister before I ran away, mainly because she was young, and I didn't know how to interact with her. I felt bad I left her here alone, but everyone loved her so I figured she would be okay. Whether she knew she had a brother, I had no idea. Did they talk about me? I presumed my mother did, so she probably had heard my name.

But I wasn't here to see her—I was here to stop the destruction of my people.

I presumed Byron would go after the Sirians at some point, as we weren't human, and he hated me the most. He wanted to see me suffer, and while home was never warm and welcoming, I didn't want to see it destroyed.

Feeling a hand slipping into my own, I found Cor smiling at me. "It will be all right. We're here with you."

I grinned. "Yeah, I know. I'm not that scared kid anymore. We have to do this—we have to get them to go after Byron before it's too late. I just don't know if anyone will listen to me. Even my own mother always seemed to shrug off anything I said as a kid."

"Well, don't forget. I can be pretty convincing myself."

That was for sure, but I didn't know how well my mother would respond to his antics or whether she cared he was a Kausian. She had fallen for a human though, so perhaps she wasn't as narrow-minded as the rest of them.

At least one could hope.

I didn't know if I wanted to tell her that he was my boyfriend or not. I didn't think she would be upset or anything, but I still wasn't sure if we were that official. I also didn't want her to believe I had been seduced by him and was being fed lies. No, I would simply explain how they were friends that I had met along the way and were also wronged by Byron. And all of that was true, as he was the one behind everything wrong with this world.

I glanced back to make sure Ellie and Zach hadn't gotten lost. They appeared to be keeping up with us well enough. They knew better than to get lost in a place like this.

The palace was a maze, to say the least, but it was a maze that I had loved as a kid. I'd found plenty of places to hide from folks, and sometimes I could go days without seeing anyone. Even the guards had trouble finding me, as there weren't too many throughout the palace—just mainly at the front gate and outside in the water. There, of course, were some scattered throughout and posted outside whatever room my mother was in. But for the most part, they kept to themselves and didn't bother with me. I wasn't sure if that was because they didn't want to guard me, but at least they weren't bullying me like many of the officials that visited my mother.

Part of the ridiculous maze that made up my home was all the stairwells. There were ones on either side of the palace and a grand one in the middle that led up to the banquet hall and to my mother's throne room. I definitely had very strong legs as a kid as there were no elevators like there were up on Zynon. I wasn't sure why elevators weren't installed down here and presumed because of how moist it was or because of some of the safety mechanisms that were in place for letting water in. Either way, our legs were going to hurt the first couple of days we were here.

The palace decor always left me in awe, even as a kid. Although it was all reinforced with steel and thick glass, much of the inner decor was made of different types of marble. The marble put in the throne room was a light beige color and had many different ocean creatures carved into it. When I was little, I had named many of these creatures and considered them to be some of my greatest companions—along with my stuffed animals, of course.

We came up to the throne room. The doors were painted like the ocean outside with giant whales swimming around. A couple of guards were stationed outside her door. The moment they saw us, they scoffed a little, but they didn't hesitate to open the door as they knew we were coming.

My mother charged at me, which was impressive as she wore a long pearl-colored robe that dragged on the floor. I hardly was able to get both feet into the room when her arms wrapped around me. She nearly choked me.

"My son! My dear son! You are finally home!"

The familiar salty, floral scent of her hair made something inside my heart feel a bit warmer. I had almost completely forgotten the smell of her perfume and shampoo. Had I really tried that hard to block all my memories of home out of my mind? Perhaps I did.

I squeezed her tight. "It's good to see you, Mom. Have you been well?"

"Of course, my darling Riri. I couldn't be happier. Other than worrying about my son day and night."

I knew she was going to play the guilt card. Granted, it wasn't her fault I left, but I had to run away before Byron could try to kill me, not that it really stopped him

—only delayed him. "I'm sorry for making you worry, but I was sort of in hiding from someone…"

I glanced over to Cor, who appeared to be holding back a laugh. I knew he was going to make fun of my nickname now. Ellie and Zach fidgeted with their shirts, glancing all around as if they didn't feel they were welcome there. I probably should have left them outside so I could talk to my mother, but there was the fact that the guards wouldn't have liked that and could have harassed them even if they were my guests.

My mother stepped back—her dark eyes going wide. "Hiding? From whom? Who would want to hurt you?"

She was as clueless as ever. How she was able to get through the fifteen years that I was here without noticing her guests spitting on me and saying awful things, I was not sure. I never brought any of it up as I didn't want to trouble her, but it ate at me that she didn't notice. I had slightly suggested a few times that people didn't like me, but she would simply reply that it was nonsense and that everyone liked me and always said great things about me.

Yeah. To her face.

But behind her back they were truly horrible. Convincing her that Byron, my own uncle, was trying to kill not only me but every race other than humans was going to take some work.

"Can we talk privately? The four of us and you?" I asked, nodding to the rest.

She glanced over my shoulder, as if she hadn't realized there were others with me. The moment she noticed them, she frowned. She must have realized what they were, and my fear of her being as bigoted as the rest of the world was correct.

"Kausians? Why did you bring Kausians with you?"

At least she didn't automatically summon the guards. I sighed. "It's a long story, Mom. But we need to talk to you alone please?"

She shook her head. "I will not be alone with these people even if they are friends of yours. Their home was destroyed for a reason, Riri. They aren't to be trusted."

I should have figured this was what was going to happen. At least she wasn't arresting them on the spot though. "Will you please give them a chance before you toss us out?"

"I wasn't going to toss you out, Riri. Just them."

I couldn't believe what I was hearing. She was going to throw my friends out simply because they were

Kausians? I rarely stood up to anyone in this place, but I would not let my mother kick them out simply because of what they were. "Where they go, I go, Mom. I won't let you kick out my friends. We have a mission to complete."

Her eyes widened, as I never argued with her or showed any sort of conflict. She glanced back at the three Kausians, who simply smiled innocently at her. She eventually turned back to me.

"Fine. They can stay. But I'm not going to hold council alone with them. If you need to talk privately with me, let us talk later tonight. I want to hold a banquet for your return."

"And my friends?" I asked.

She glanced over at them, frowning. "They can come, but they better stay out of trouble, you understand?"

"Of course, Mother. They will be on their best behavior. Just like always."

I swore I heard Cor cough when I said that, but as I glanced at him, he wasn't doing or saying anything—simply waiting for this conversation to finish. I had a feeling convincing my mother about everything that had happened was going to take a long longer than I hoped.

# CHAPTER VI

Gabe

"I'm sorry what she said about Kausians. That was unjust and rude," I commented to Cor, Ellie, and Zach as we made it back to my room. Luckily, I had a suite with two bedrooms, a large bathroom, and a nice living area, so we didn't have to worry about being separated. Why I grew up with two bedrooms was unknown to me. Perhaps my mother thought I could bring over friends, not that I had any. Well, there was one boy who sometimes slept over, but he wasn't exactly what I would call a friend so much as someone who wanted free food and to do whatever he wanted.

"Don't worry about it," Zach commented as we made our way down the familiar corridors. "We're used to it. And we know you aren't like that and how you were probably treated much the same growing up." He glanced around. "Besides the whole living in style."

I let out a laugh. "Yeah, I'm glad I had a nice place growing up. It was easy to hide in here from everything. And I had whatever I wanted."

Cor slapped my back. "But it doesn't make up for being treated as if you were trash. We get it." His lips curled into a smile. "Riri."

I rolled my eyes as the other two laughed. "I knew you were going to bring that up."

He squeezed my cheeks. "It's just such a cute nickname, how could I not? Maybe I should start calling you that."

I shook my head. "Please don't—only my mother calls me that, and it would be weird."

"I'm kidding. I know it would be weird. Besides, I like calling you Gabe, among other things."

I felt my cheeks blush a little. I prayed he didn't say some of those names out loud for the others to hear.

They didn't seem to notice as we began to make our way up the stairs.

My room was near the middle of the palace, with my mother's room almost near the top. We had quite a few flights to go, but since most of us were used to being on the run, we were at least in shape. As we stared at the last flight, I realized it had been a while since I had walked so much, as I was used to taking trains and sitting in casinos. Perhaps I should work on that.

We made it to the level of my bedroom and the familiar dark walls with white flecks of marble decorated part of the corridor. The rest was glass that peered out into the ocean. The familiar blue welcomed me like a home that should have made me feel comfortable, yet it felt colder than any hotel or casino we stayed at. A school of fish passed by the window, and I watched as Zach and Ellie pressed their faces on the glass and observed them go by.

"Really you guys," Cor commented. "What are you, children?"

Zach turned to face him. "Hey, this could be our only chance to see stuff like this! I'm going to take in all that I can."

"You realize you can swim underwater, right? You

could just go swim to somewhere to see fish."

Zach stuck his tongue out. "It's not the same! Clearly!"

"Whatever. Just don't embarrass us, will you?"

Ellie was second to stick her tongue out at Cor and stepped away from the glass. I noted her cheeks blushing as she followed behind Cor. Something about their familiarity ate at me. It wasn't fair—I wished I had a relationship like that growing up. But I didn't. I was completely alone.

I led them all to my room. The door creaked as I opened it, as if no one had been there since I had left—everything about me completely forgotten.

The main area was large and looked out into the ocean. The floor was made of a bluish granite with metallic dark walls. There were a couple of off-white couches and a table in the middle. There were two bedrooms connected to the main area, mine on the right and the other room to the left. I gulped as the room felt familiar and yet so foreign to me. I wasn't the same person when I left here, and now that I was back, I was realizing that more and more.

"Nice place," Zach commented as he glanced around. "Which room is ours?"

I pointed at the guest room. "Your room is that one. There is also a nice bathroom with a large bath."

He nodded. "Sweet. Thanks. Also, do you get room service? Is it called that when you live here?" He rubbed his stomach. "I'm starving and would love something to eat."

Ellie shook her head. "Are you serious? Is food all you think about?"

"You can't tell me that you aren't hungry."

"I don't let my stomach dictate what I do."

As she said that, her stomach grumbled.

Zach pointed at her. "See! You are hungry!"

"Fine," she sighed. "I admit, I'm hungry, but we really need to discuss what we should do from here on out. I mean, we aren't going to get anything done at the banquet tonight. Your mother may say she will meet with you later, but do you honestly believe that? Or do you think she will keep pushing the conversation back?"

She had a point. We really needed to get this thing moving, and my mom was one to push any serious conversation back. "It's almost as if you could read her mind. Yes, she tends to put things off, not wanting to hear the truth. I think coming here might have been a bad idea."

"It's the only shot we have for getting an army to help us take down Byron. And we really didn't have anywhere else to go," Cor commented. "Could you try to see her before the banquet? Force her to talk to you?"

I shrugged. "I could try. But I can't make any promises."

Cor clapped his hands. "Then let's do that. But first let's order food, wash up, and change into something fancier. I have a feeling we stand out in these clothes."

We all nodded, and I went to the intercom, hoping that it still worked after all this time.

Cor was right—I felt a lot better after taking a bath and getting some food in me.

I felt refreshed, especially after changing into some silk robes and clean socks and shoes. It had been a while since I had worn anything so extravagant. Most Sirians wore clothes similar to humans, but some still wore their traditional-style clothing, mainly in the palace. I was able to get some guards to get clothes for the others. They weren't as fancy as mine, as I was the prince after all, but it would do for tonight.

I finished tying the last knot when Cor came into the

room. He was wearing an all-black robe. I gave him a whistle. "Well, well, don't you look stylish?"

He grinned. "I can pull off any type of clothes, yes. It's such a cruel punishment to be this handsome."

I stepped up to him and traced my finger on the edge of the fabric. "I just can't wait to take you out of these. You have no idea how much it turns me on, seeing you wear my culture's clothes."

Cor lifted my chin a little and kissed me. "Why wait? It's not like we're in any real hurry."

I moved back and shook my head. "No, these are too much of a pain to put back on. Besides, I want to try to go find my mother."

"I suppose you're right. And what exactly should I do in the meantime?"

I shrugged. "Stay out of trouble. I mean, I doubt you would be able to seduce your way into getting information here. It would be safest if you stayed put."

"Stay put, huh? That's not something I'm good at."

I couldn't help but smile a little at that comment. "Just… don't cause trouble, all right? We want my mother to trust you."

"Fine." Cor collapsed on the bed. "I'll try. But I can't promise anything."

I rolled my eyes. "You really can't survive five seconds without some kind of drama or adventure, can you?"

"What's that supposed to mean?"

"Oh, a lot of things. First off, there is the fact you haven't answered my question about Ellie. Then second, you had a whole other job with Krax, didn't you? Admit it. You were working for him."

Cor frowned as he turned to me. "This isn't the time or place—"

"When is the time or place, Cor? You are always making up excuses. I don't know if you noticed, but we're in the thick of it. We may not get out of this alive, and you won't tell me whether you love me more than you love her."

He was silent for a moment. "I don't know what you want from me, Gabe. I love you—you know that. We have always had an open relationship. Why is it bothering you so much?"

I took a deep breath and let it out slowly, trying to calm myself down. How could he be so narrow-minded? "Because never before had anything you'd done have to do with love. Yeah, you slept with others, but that was for money—it had nothing to do with marriage or wanting to spend your life with someone else. So, I need to know, was I just a means to an end? Or did you really have feelings for me?"

Cor stood up. "I care about you, Gabe. Nothing will change that. I just— I didn't…" He scratched the back of his head. "I don't know. I didn't think this far ahead. I figured when I killed Krax's family I would be executed on the spot. That's all I wanted in life— revenge. But now things are different. I haven't had a chance to think that far ahead. I'm sorry, but that's the truth. I won't have an answer for you until this is all over."

I frowned. It wasn't exactly what I wanted to hear, but at least it was something. "Well, while you think about it, I'm going to go convince my mother she needs to lead an army against Byron."

With that, I turned toward the door and headed to my mother's chambers.

# CHAPTER VII

Ellie

I almost fell straight on my ass as Gabe opened the door to his room. And by almost, I meant I did. It hurt—a lot—as the floor was made out of some kind of blue marble. I scooted back a bit, acted like I was just hanging out. On the floor. In nice clothing. Minding my own business and not listening in on Cor and Gabe's conversation.

All right, maybe I was listening in, but I couldn't help it—I had originally ventured over here to get help with my robe as I didn't know what rope and piece of cloth went where. Then I heard arguing. Then I thought I had heard my name.

Of which I did. Because they were talking about Cor's and my relationship. I wasn't even sure what I felt for Cor anymore, and I was better at figuring out my emotions than he ever was. Cor always pushed his emotions away and tried to be happy and adventurous all the time. I wondered if he ever really sat still long enough to do some self-reflection. I couldn't say for certain, as we hadn't seen each other for three years, but I had a feeling he hadn't. He only thought about revenge and focused on his hatred. Granted, I did too, but at least I took some time to learn about myself as well.

Gabe didn't say anything or even look at me as he went out the door toward his mother's room. I slowly stood up, but not before Cor stepped into the living room. He was wearing an all-black robe similar to what Gabe was wearing. He looked dashing, but I wouldn't admit that. It would boost his ego way too much.

Cor folded his arms and leaned against the doorway. "Were you listening in?"

I patted any dirt that was on me. There was none as

the floors were quite clean. It was just a force of habit. "I don't know what you mean. I would never listen in on a private conversation."

"Mm-hmm. And how many times did you get in trouble for listening in when your father was meeting with the officials of town?"

I shrugged, the memories coming back to me. My father's face used to be able to get such a bright red. "Maybe like twice?"

He laughed. "Yeah, a month. Once, he found you in the cupboard and you tried to say you were searching for your pet mouse."

"I thought he would believe that one."

"The fact he knew you were afraid of mice was probably the giveaway." He chuckled some more. "Anyway, have any ideas on what we should do next?"

"Stay here, just like Gabe said."

Cor raised an eyebrow. "I thought you said you weren't listening in?"

I stuck my tongue out at him. "Whatever. I may have overheard a couple of things. I think waiting until he comes back would be best. It's not as if we're really welcome here."

"Are we welcomed anywhere?"

"Well no, but in this case I don't want to be thrown into some dungeon in the palace. This room is quite nice after all."

He nodded slowly, but his eyes seemed distant, as if he was thinking about something else. After a moment, he blinked and his attention came back to me. "You look nice, by the way. Green suits you. But you're wearing that all wrong."

I sighed. "That's why I was coming over to your room. I need help putting the rest on."

His lips curled. "Are you saying you like having me dress you?"

I felt my cheeks get warm. "No, you are just more experienced in proper clothes than Zach and I are."

"Mm-hmm."

"Ugh. Whatever. Just help me fix it. Zach is still changing in our room. Can you fix it in Gabe's room?"

"Of course." Cor led me into Gabe's room. The granite floor in there was a dark blue, compared to the lighter color in the living area. The bed had dark black blankets and sheets. It seemed darker than what I would assume Gabe would like, but then again, he liked Cor and he tended to wear dark clothes, just as Cor was now.

Cor moved me through the room in front of the long mirror. I stared at myself, feeling like a mess. I should know how to dress myself, but these proper clothes were so hard. Why couldn't they be easier? Don't rich people want easier things?

"Okay, so first," he began as he untied the sash. "You folded the robe wrong. It goes right over left for women who are single. Then you need to leave a bit of slack from your neck like so."

I felt his fingers on the back of my neck, which sent shivers down my spine. I shouldn't have felt like this, but I couldn't help it. He had been my one and only love—he was one of my best friends growing up. We had been inseparable. Then that friendship became something more, and I just couldn't shake this feeling of wanting him close constantly.

It was much different with Zach. I liked being with him and hanging out. We even snuggle more often than not, but it wasn't the same. I didn't want him sexually close but more just there as a friend. With Cor though, I knew I couldn't just cuddle and not have it lead to something else. It was fiery and passionate. Zach was more familial.

Cor slipped in front of me and smiled as he tied the

belt. "And you tie this like so. Easy peasy."

I glanced up to find Cor's golden eyes staring down at me. His white hair was purposely messy, per the norm, which contrasted with his dark robes. I bit my lips as I looked up at him. Even though we had been separated for only three years, he had matured a lot since I had last seen him. Maybe even grown a couple of inches.

We stood like that for a long moment, simply taking each other in. Cor licked his pink lips as he glanced down at my own. I felt frozen in place, not sure if I should move away or keep standing there, hoping for what might come next.

He slowly reached down to my cheek. I didn't hesitate but let him move closer to me, his lips inches away from my own. I knew I shouldn't—I knew there was still a lot we needed to deal with—but I wanted to feel his lips on mine again.

Our lips touched, and I could taste the sweet flavor of mint and cinnamon. His hands ran up my back, and I grabbed the edge of his robe and pulled him closer. I didn't want this moment to end—I wanted this to last forever.

But I knew that was wrong. I knew I needed to stop

and discuss our relationship with him. We needed to figure out how we really felt about each other and how Gabe fit into the picture. I didn't want to destroy their relationship when it seemed like they both really cared for each other.

Except the two of us had also once cared for each other. We had been engaged and wanted a life together. And while I had blamed him for the destruction of Kaus, I really hadn't known the truth. I hadn't known he was set up and that he was just trying to build a life for the two of us.

Where would we be if he hadn't betrayed us like that? What kind of life could we have lived if there hadn't been these prejudices in the world?

Cor pushed me back onto the bed, his lips not leaving my own. I scooted back a little as he placed his knees on both sides of my waist.

"Hey Ellie, can you help me with this hair…" I heard Zach's voice come from the entrance. He immediately shook his head when he saw the two of us. "Are you guys serious?"

Cor was off me in nanoseconds, which really reminded me of old times. I also stood up and quickly commented, "It's not what it looks like!"

Zach rolled his eyes. "Oh really. It looks like you were making out and maybe a bit more while we're in the middle of dealing with an all-out genocide." He shook his head. "You two are ridiculous. After everything, are you really putting all of us in jeopardy?"

"Zach…"

"Forget it. I need to get some fresh air or whatever." Zach hurried toward the front door and entered the corridor, slamming the door behind himself. I went to run after him when Cor grabbed my wrist.

"Wait. We aren't supposed to leave the room."

"I can't let Zach run off like that. He could get lost or a guard might arrest him or something, not knowing Gabe brought him here."

"That's his own fault. He can't deal with our relationship. He never could."

I shook my head. "You may be cunning, Cor, but sometimes you can be a real jackass. I'm going to go get him and bring him back before he does something stupid. I hope you'll help me find him."

Cor went to the door. "He can't be that fast." He opened it, and we both looked out. There was no sign of Zach. Cor sighed. "You've got to be kidding me. Where did he go?"

I glanced both ways again, hoping to see any trace of Zach. There was none. He could have gone either way. "I'll go right and you go left. If you can't find him, come back here in an hour, okay?"

Cor let out an exasperated sigh. "Whatever. Fine. But if this all causes more problems, it's your fault."

I shot him a look from the corner of my eye. "I beg to differ."

# CHAPTER VIII

Cor

This was not my fault, so why did I have to deal with it?

Zach was the one who'd run off, and now we were searching for him in this palace, which could get us in a heap of trouble. Granted, I was going to go sneak around later before Gabe came back already, but now I was being forced to walk around, which wasn't okay. Zach just needed to chill and not cause so much drama all the time.

Perhaps I was annoyed that Zach made things with Ellie end sooner than I would have preferred. It had been years since I'd gotten to kiss her and touch her, so maybe I was taking those frustrations out on him. Then again, he had always been like this—making comments, not liking that Ellie and I were intimate. I never understood what his problem was. Perhaps he didn't like the change in our friendship dynamic.

I didn't care one way or another who Zach liked or didn't like, as long as it didn't get in my way. I didn't see how there was a problem with being both with Ellie and Gabe, as they both wanted to be with me. That much was clear.

But was it for the better? Were they happy? It seemed like they were happy and that they didn't mind each other, so why couldn't we all be together? I had been with plenty of people while dating Gabe, so it was no big deal. If they wanted to leave, they could make that decision on their own. It shouldn't be up to me.

If I had to choose, however, I didn't know what to do. I doubted it would come to that, as I doubted any of us were going to make it out alive. Byron was strong and smart. There was no way we were going to win this without giving up our lives in the process. Or at least I didn't see any other way.

Deciding to search on the next floor, I headed down the stairs and glanced around for Zach. He wasn't there, nor was there anyone around. This spot wasn't near where we had met with the queen, so I presumed there wouldn't be many guards up here anyway. But it was still a lot quieter than I would assume a palace to be. Where were all the dignitaries and guests? Was that not a common thing in the Sirian Zone? Was this a quiet time of the year for the palace and normal? I wasn't sure.

Or perhaps with Gabe back, all the guards and people were planning something together and going to attack us all.

Stopping in my tracks, I sighed. That was totally what was going to happen, wasn't it? We were going to get set up. I could feel it.

Once we were done looking for Zach, I most definitely was going to search for any signs of Byron and see if he had some connection there. Although he was Gabe's uncle, I had really doubted anyone here would have anything to do with him. Perhaps I was wrong—perhaps he twisted their minds just like they had the Silurians. If that were the case, we were screwed.

Why did I have a feeling that was the case? I sighed as I leaned my head back and stretched. I needed to come up with a plan, not to mention see if I could find any proof of my suspicion. Then, if I was right, we would get the hell out of here.

So while I was out looking for Zach, I would also look for clues. Easy peasy. If anyone asked what I was up to, I would just explain how I was lost and was looking for Gabe. If that would work.

Gabe's mom didn't seem happy he was with Kausians. It wasn't surprising, but I was surprised that Gabe didn't tell his mom that we were dating. I thought he would have at least said something to help her understand why he trusted us, but I guess that wasn't the case. At least he stood his ground and didn't let her kick us out. Hopefully she wouldn't send her guards on us behind his back.

As I ventured through the corridor, I wished I had seen a map of the palace. That would have made all this easier. Then I would know where I was going, and I would know where to look or at least have a better idea where to look. I wondered if I could get my hands on one. Perhaps I could find a guard room or something, but that would make them suspicious of me if I got caught.

I wished there was one day in my life that was easy.

I hadn't had a day where I didn't think about what my next move was—what I needed to do to push forward—for what seemed like ever. Had there been a day where I wasn't looking over my back or making sure we were safe?

Even as a kid I had to make sure there weren't people tailing me while I was in different zones. Ellie, Zach, and I used to sneak out quite often, getting into trouble wherever we went. We usually made it out unscathed although we had quite a few wanted posters up in establishments. Those would eventually come down and we would go back and harass them even more. It sounded counterintuitive, but when that was what was expected of us, we didn't really care at the time.

It seemed things didn't change.

Rubbing my eyes, I realized how tired I truly was. I wanted it all to be over—I wanted to finally be on the other side of this. I wanted…

I didn't know what I wanted. I didn't know if I wanted a life with Ellie or a life with Gabe. For my entire life, I had envisioned a future with Ellie. I was supposed to go to college, get a real job as a teacher or in some line of business. Then I was tricked, and that future was taken away from me. After everything that had happened, I figured Ellie would be too mad to ever love me again.

Then I met Gabe, and he was so sweet and cute. We both were running away from something and could relate to one another. We both had similar goals and wanted to prove people wrong about us. I loved him, but it was different than the love I had for Ellie. I just didn't know. I wanted them both but wasn't sure if that was even possible.

As I rounded a corner, I found the familiar red hair of Zach. He was looking out at the ocean, clearly lost in thought. I watched as he stared at the black-and-white fish that swam in front of the glass. As I stepped up to him, he turned and saw me, then rolled his eyes.

"Great. You found me."

I shrugged. "Yeah, well, you ran off like a child, and Ellie got worried."

He rolled his eyes. "I'm just sick of you trying to wrap everyone around your finger."

I let out a laugh. "Excuse me?"

"Admit it, Cor, you don't actually know how to love

—you just want everyone to love you. You aren't able to put other's needs ahead of your own. You are just stringing both Gabe and Ellie along because you want to feel needed, but you can't even put yourself in their shoes and understand why they are frustrated. You know this is going to end horribly for all of you, and you don't do anything to fix it."

There was a lot to unpack there. "I'm not stringing them along. They can leave whenever they want, but they don't. I love them both. I just… I don't know who I want to be with."

"So you keep pulling at both their heart strings. How romantic."

I ran my hands through my hair. "Look, I'm not getting into this with you. It's none of your business, to be frank."

He folded his arms in front of himself. "Seriously? Who do you think was there to pick up the pieces when you left us? Who do you think was there when she wouldn't stop crying? Hell, we've known her the same length of time. It is my business—she's my friend."

I didn't like thinking about how much it must have broken Ellie's heart that I ran away. At the time, I had thought it was the best course of action, as the journey ahead for me was going to be one full of blood and revenge. I didn't want to drag her into such things. I also didn't want to admit the truth to her even if I had been used. I didn't want her to look at me with anger and pity. So I left her behind, hoping she would find a better life for herself.

Now I knew that was wrong, but one couldn't change the past, only the future. That was why I moved forward and why I would do what I needed to do to make things right.

Which meant I would have to take down Byron even if it was the last thing I did.

I shook my head. "Don't you dare. You have no idea what I've been through. I was trying to build a life for us—give her something no one else could have. Then I was betrayed. Do you think it was easy? Do you think that I didn't feel horrible? That I didn't experience heartbreak? I was broken, and there was no one to help me pick up the pieces."

"Oh yeah?" Zach stepped forward. "And whose fault was that? If you had told us the truth, we could have helped you. We had been friends all our lives, and you tossed us aside as if you didn't need us anymore. Don't act like a martyr, Cor. You had people to help, and you decided to hang yourself."

I didn't say anything, mainly because I knew he was right. Life would have gone much differently if I had come clean right away. Perhaps we would have gone somewhere else to live and not gone after Krax. Or perhaps we would have figured out the truth behind Byron before this. Or perhaps we would all be dead. There was no way of knowing.

Zach simply shook his head and stepped past me but not without bumping into my shoulder.

"I'm heading back to the suite. You should head back too. Or not. I really don't care."

With that, he left me standing there. There were so many things I wanted to say to Zach, but I felt most of them would just make the situation worse. I took a deep breath and went back to what I really wanted to do—find evidence that may save our asses. Then maybe Zach would choke on his words about me not caring about them.

# CHAPTER IX

Gabe

My mother was nowhere to be found.

I sighed. Where could she be? She wasn't in her room or the throne room. It wasn't as if the palace was small, but I figured I would find her by now.

Most of the palace seemed to be the same since I had left. A lot of the decor and coldness still remained. The only difference was that the guards weren't making comments or giving me that nasty of looks as they used to. I figured it was because they didn't remember me, or perhaps they figured ignoring me would make me go away. That was what the few who were outside my mother's room and throne room had done.

Other than those few guards, there weren't many others out surveilling the corridors. I wasn't sure why that was, but I was thankful as I didn't want to deal with anyone else. I wanted my time here to come to a close so I could go back to Mu.

And then what?

I knew the plan was to stop Byron, but once we got my mother to turn on him, what was next? Would we simply let everything happen on its own, or would we be in the thick of it, also fighting? I wasn't much of a fighter and didn't know the first thing about dueling or shooting a gun. I would probably have to remedy that soon if we were indeed going to be a part of this war.

Even if I survived it all, I didn't know what I was going to do with myself. Was I going to come back here? I didn't particularly want to as these walls haunted me. Even though this place was large, I felt constricted and wanted to run as far as I could. But if I went back to Mu, what would I have? Would I still be with Cor and his friends? Or would they toss me aside now that dealing with the Sirians was over?

I couldn't imagine them just casting me aside like used garbage, as they were quite kind. But I also didn't see where I came to play in their dynamic. Was I the charming one who could pay for anything they wished? Was that why they truly kept me around?

Those thoughts plagued my mind as I rounded a corner. I felt something ram straight into my leg. Glancing down, I found a little girl on the ground. I must have run into her as I wasn't paying much attention to my surroundings.

"Oh no, are you all right?" I asked as I bent down to her.

The little girl was wearing a pink robe with a lavender belt and white rope. Her hair was dark and braided back with a flower that matched her robe. Her dark eyes were beginning to water, and her face was turning red. Before she could start crying, she took a deep breath.

"I can't cry. I'm a princess. I must keep my emotions hidden."

Her voice was sweet and light. I smiled as I realized it was my little sister whom I had bumped into. "Princess? Then are you little Kishiko?"

She grinned. "I am? Who are you?"

So she didn't remember, which was fair since I didn't remember her. I helped her up. "You have grown up to be a beautiful little girl."

She curtsied. "Thank you, but you didn't answer my question about who you are."

Darn. She noticed. "Well, I um…" I didn't know if I should tell her the truth or not. Did she know she had a big brother? Or was I painted as some kind of monster? I honestly didn't want to know the truth as it would break my heart to see such a young girl be corrupted by society. But I knew I shouldn't lie to her. "I'm your big brother."

Her eyes widened, and any memory of her recent injury was gone. "You can't be him! Are you Riri?"

So she did know my name or at least what my mother called me. "I am."

Kishiko jumped up and down. "My brother! I finally get to see my brother! Pick me up! Pick me up!"

I did as she asked, and she smiled in glee. "Yay!"

I laughed. She was the most adorable thing in the entire world. I regretted not being here to watch her grow up, but I knew I'd had to leave for my own mental health. I didn't believe I would have survived if I had stayed down here.

"Well, where should I take you, my princess?"

"Can you take me to my room? That's where I was heading since I have to get ready for the banquet tonight."

Even at her young age, she was expected to engage in such banquets. I remembered having to do the same when I was little. I hated every minute of it, although I had a feeling her experience was different than mine. She would probably be ordered to retire early, only needing to appear to keep the people happy. In most cases, folks liked children.

"Sure. Which way do I need to head?" It wasn't as if I had gone to her room that often, as I had kept my distance from most people by the time she was born. I wasn't jealous or anything, I just didn't want to deal with anyone.

She pointed down the hall. "That way."

I started toward the way she gestured. She kept moving in my arms, fidgeting as if she were excited. This made me smile even though I kept feeling as if I were going to drop her. Hopefully I wouldn't as I didn't want to bring any harm to her, intentional or not.

I was glad to be part of her life even if it were for only a second. I would cherish this moment if it was the only time I got to be with her. I knew I had to protect this kingdom—if not for my people, then just for her. She would grow up to be strong like our mother and be the best ruler there could be.

We made it to her room, and I set her down on the pinkish marble floor. The room was similar to mine in size but decorated completely differently. She apparently loved pink flowers and sea creatures as she had what appeared to be a hundred stuffed animals. It was the complete opposite of my dark moody room, and I felt it suited her perfectly.

Kishiko ran over to a dolphin plushy and grabbed it. "This is my favorite stuffed animal!"

"Is it?" I asked. "Dolphins are pretty cool. I swam with a couple myself when I was younger."

"Really? That's so cool! Mother won't let me go out and swim by myself yet, and I hate swimming with guards."

So did I, but I had a feeling it was for two completely different reasons. "When you get older, you'll have a bit more freedom."

"I sure hope so." She clutched her dolphin tight. "I think, since you love them so much too, you should have my stuffed animal."

I laughed as I knelt down. She was still clutching it, so I doubted she really wanted me to take it, not that I would. "Thank you very much, but I can't take this. It's your favorite toy. Besides, I won't be here for that long, and I can't exactly take anything like this with me. I would be too afraid to lose it."

Her lips pouted. "You are leaving me again?"

It felt like an arrow had gone through my heart. I shouldn't have said I was going to leave, but I didn't exactly want to get her hopes up that I was staying. "I'm sorry. But there is a lot going on. You'll understand when you get older."

She pouted some more and clutched her dolphin. "You sound like Mother. She says that about anything she doesn't want to explain. I just want to be older so I can understand everything that's going on."

I chuckled. "Believe me, you don't. The years will pass by quickly, and then you'll wish for your childhood again."

She sighed. "That's also what Mother says."

Although I wanted to keep spending time with her, as I didn't know when I would get to see her again, I knew I needed to talk to my mother before the event tonight. "Speaking of Mother, do you know where she is?"

She nodded. "Yup. She's in the kitchen, talking to the chefs about tonight's dinner."

Of course she was. I should have figured. My stomach grumbled at the thought of all the delicious food there would be this evening even though I had just eaten.

"Thank you. I'll see you later tonight then, okay?"

Her eyes grew wide as she went over to her shelves. She started rummaging through her games and toys. "Wait, why won't you play with me some more?"

I walked over and patted her head where there were no braids to mess up. "How about I promise to play after tonight? And then maybe I'll read you a story before you go to bed?"

Her dark eyes lit up. "Really? Any story I want?"

I chuckled. "Sure. So until then, think about which story you want me to read and I'll go find our mother so I can talk to her about some urgent business."

"Okay!"

I gave her a hug and then headed out the door toward the kitchen. If I remembered correctly, the kitchen was down a couple of floors. I snapped and clapped my hands as I ventured down the hallway. There weren't many guards stationed at all. It was strange.

Something was up. I glanced around but didn't see anything off. It was as if my intuition was screaming at me, but I had no reason to actually feel that way. Was it years of abuse in these halls, or was there something really there?

I had always felt the same as a kid, although there sometimes were people around the corner, wanting to pick on me. I couldn't tell if this feeling was something residual or if I needed to be alert. There was no way Byron would have made it down here already, but could there be someone else after me?

As I rounded a corner, I felt something go over my face. Apparently I was right.

I flailed my arms and tried to punch whoever it was, but it was no use. There was more than one of them, and they grabbed my arms and tied them behind my back. I felt something jab into my side.

"Walk forward, nice and easy."

Great. This was all I needed.

# CHAPTER X

Ellie

Where was he? Why did Zach run off like that?

Zach, Cor, and I had known each other for quite some time. Then when Cor and I started dating, he felt uneasy around us. He became distant, and although we did a lot together, he didn't seem to enjoy it as much as he had before then. I never asked him about it as I was young and stupid and wasn't sure what was going on. Also, perhaps, I was more thinking about Cor and our life together. I wanted Zach there too, of course, but I dreamed of marriage and having a family with Cor. I should have asked though, but even if he was sometimes distant, he never lashed out like this.

Then again, after everything we had gone through, it was probably a mistake to kiss Cor. I had missed him. And part of me still dreamed of the future we were supposed to have.

That future was taken away from us. I shouldn't keep wishing for it. I needed to move on. I needed to help save the world.

Just like the world tried to help us in our time of need.

It didn't. No one helped us. They watched as our world was destroyed. They threw us in the mud, didn't help any refugees. They treated us like garbage. Why should we help them? Why shouldn't we let them destroy each other? Then whoever is left of the Kausians can inherit the world.

If there were many of us left, that was.

I wasn't even sure how many Kausians were left. I had run into a couple of them over the years. They were afraid—hiding in the shadows and praying that no one would notice them. Although we tended to keep to the shadows when Kaus was still standing, it was a bit different now. Now we knew there was no home to go back to.

Letting a long breath out, I knew I couldn't just let this slide. Innocent people would be caught in the middle, not to mention the person we needed to stop was the person who destroyed my kind. Whether I truly wanted to help others or if it was because I wanted to make him pay, I wasn't sure.

As I turned down the next hallway, I saw a group of men surrounding someone. I quickly backed up around the corner so they wouldn't notice me. I knew better than to get into a fight here, especially when there was no easy way to leave this zone. I debated if I should turn and pretend I hadn't seen anything. I knew it wasn't Zach as I would have seen a flash of his red hair. But was I certain of that?

On the other hand, how many times had I gotten roped into the middle of other people's affairs simply because I decided to step in to save the day? Sometimes I was just in the vicinity and people decided to take me down with them. No, I should just walk away and keep searching for Zach.

But it wouldn't hurt to get a peek of what was going on. A group of four guards had a bag over someone's head. Did someone break in? If they were breaking in, they definitely had chosen the wrong set of clothes as what they were wearing wasn't good for sneaking around in. The person was wearing a light aquamarine robe that was long and ornate. Then it hit me. I knew that clothing.

It was Gabe.

Why would his own people capture him like that? The people surrounding him were definitely guards as they were wearing the same uniform as the ones at the front had been. Whether they stole them or were actually guards, I had no idea. Either way, it was apparent they were with Byron.

We were in trouble.

How did he find us? How did he already know where we were headed? Did he send out an alert the moment we left to everyone? Or had he known we were headed this way?

Or had the guards been alerted a long time ago to kidnap Gabe if he ever went home?

That was the constant fear that Gabe lived with. That was why he'd run away. Although different circumstances, I understood what he went through. We were constantly targeted wherever we went.

But first thing was first, I had to get Gabe out of this. I had to figure out how to take them out and get him to safety.

I cursed under my breath. This wasn't going to be easy—not with so many guards and the fact I did not have my gun on me. Granted, I had three knives, which would give me some advantage, but it wasn't as easy to stop someone with a knife as it was with a gun. What I needed was Cor or Zach to back me up, but I had neither at the moment.

Where could they be?

I didn't know this palace that well, so going to find them and then trying to figure out where these men were taking Gabe wouldn't be the best plan. Biting my lip, I knew what I needed to do—I had to follow these men, figure out where they were going to take Gabe, then go get some backup. If I charged in now, a lot of problems could arise. We all needed to come up with a plan.

Staying as far behind the guards as I could without losing sight of them, I ventured down the corridor, careful to be quiet and unseen. They kept checking behind their backs, which made me have to hop quickly between places to hide. Luckily there were quite a few large vases on this level, along with some statues and whatnot. Thank goodness rich people like this loved to decorate.

They made their way to one of the side stairwells and led Gabe down the stairs. I couldn't imagine that was easy being blindfolded. I quietly followed them down. The sound of their steps echoed in the stairwell, so as long as I could hear them, I knew they were going down the stairs.

The tricky part was following them without them hearing me.

I only went down a couple of steps before I realized it would be best if I hiked up my robe. The shoes Gabe had given me had a soft sole, luckily, so I didn't make a sound as I stepped. I was careful to watch how fast I was going so that I didn't come up on them but also didn't want to lag so far behind that I didn't know which exact floor they got off at.

We passed floor after floor, and I did my best to keep from breathing heavily. It had been a while since I climbed a steep hill and even longer since I used this many stairs. My legs were going to hurt tomorrow.

I eventually heard the sound of their steps and Gabe's struggles stop. I quickened my pace and checked the third and second floor to find that they weren't there. Hurrying to the first floor, I found them guiding Gabe down the hall. I hid behind a statue and watched as they opened a door and entered.

So that was where they were going to keep him.

Now the question was who in the world orchestrated all this? Had it been Byron, or did Gabe have more big enemies than he thought? I had to hope it was Byron for the sake of all this staying a bit more simple.

I waited a little bit to see if there would be anyone leaving. No one left the room, so I had to assume they were tying him up. The fact this was the ground level would be helpful in remembering where he was as I went and searched for Zach and Cor.

As I headed back to the stairwell, I caught sight of a few of the guests who were coming in for the banquet. There was a woman who had braided her hair in shapes that disobeyed the laws of physics. I couldn't imagine how much hair spray and gel was in her hair. With her was a man with short hair with a matching dark gray robe. Both the robes also had birds depicted on them.

I could only imagine what beautiful things I would see tonight.

But that was not what I needed to focus on at that

moment. I needed to help Gabe and figure out why his own people had abducted him.

And whether we needed to get out of there as fast as we could.

# CHAPTER XI

Zach

I wasn't acting like a child, and I knew it.

That was always his insult to me. I just enjoyed keeping a childlike innocence, not to mention I loved to stay excited about things instead of so-called acting like an adult and not having joy in life.

But in this case, that wasn't what he meant. He was saying I was acting like a kid because I had run off. I didn't want to stay with him any longer. He was pissing me off, and I was afraid I would do something rash.

I just couldn't stand by and watch Ellie go through having her heart broken again. It took weeks, months even, for her to have any resemblance to living normally, if one could even call it that. I knew we had found out the truth—how Cor had been tricked—but that didn't mean I was going to stand by and watch him play with her heart all over again.

It would have been different if he didn't have another partner. But now he had Gabe, so there was no reason to be doing what he was doing. No, he was just playing a game. He didn't understand love. I doubted after everything he ever could.

Not when he had so much guilt on his conscience.

But I still shouldn't have acted so rashly. I knew it also had to do with some jealousy I had felt since I was a kid. While I didn't want a relationship like they did, I also didn't want to be excluded or forgotten by them. I always felt that they were going to go on with their lives and leave me behind. Then I would be alone. Just like I had been before Ellie came along.

Kind of like what Gabe went through as a kid.

So I understood why he was hanging on to Cor, just like Ellie, and like how I was with Ellie. None of us wanted to lose each other after everything we had been through. We were all each other's lifeline, so to speak, and after this was over, I feared the connections would change.

Problem was, would it be for the better or for the worse?

Granted, we had to survive all this first, which was easier said than done. But we would find a way to live —we always would. Whether it would mean we would win this war was another story.

I turned around another metal corridor and found I had no idea where I was. At least it was quite a beautiful hallway on this level. The marble was a blue color with lots of large orange vases and white statues. I glanced at one of the plaques of the statues and discovered it was of some politician back in the day. I wondered what sort of things he saw and did and whether he was a good person or not.

If I knew anything about politicians, probably not.

Bringing my attention back to the present, I ventured down the hallway some more. I didn't remember these colored walls on the level that Gabe was at, so I figured he wouldn't be here.

Heading up another level, I found that the walls were darker. I sort of remembered this dark of walls and figured this had to be it, although I didn't know where his room was. I sighed. I should have stayed with Cor, but I was too mad at him still. And because I figured he was pretty mad at me as well. No one likes to be called out on their toxic behavior—I knew I sure didn't. But he really needed to be as he was making a big mistake.

There was no way this was going to end well for any of them. I just didn't want to see Ellie cry again, but I had a feeling she would. And I would be there for her, just like I always was.

Stepping up to one of the glass walls, I stared out at the water. This place was really quite beautiful, as were all its people. I couldn't believe that it was all built underwater. It knew it had been hundreds of years since it was built, but its grandeur still astonished me. I wasn't good at comparing sizes and knew it was much smaller than other zone's capitals, but it was at least a quarter of the size of the human capital, which was saying a lot. There were sections that were being updated and other parts that were being expanded. If I remembered correctly, there was an underwater mine a few miles away that had a lot of this metal, of which they used here and sold up on Mu for different materials and such. Glass, of course, was made from all the sand.

I assumed that the Sirians imported some types of food, this marble, and material for different types of clothing. I wondered how much had changed when they started communicating with Mu again. I knew that at a time they had lived on the oceans but found a way to stay down here for long periods of time. It was interesting how cultures could change like that.

Until one culture was completely shunned and then destroyed because of lies.

I watched as purple and yellow fish swam close to the glass. I tapped at the glass, and the fish swam closer to where my finger was. I moved it back and forth and the fish followed it, which made me smile a bit.

The fish were more abundant here than birds on land. There were so many different types of creatures underwater, and they all fascinated me. There were small ones and large ones, and the best part about it all was that since I was behind the glass, the large ones couldn't get me. I couldn't say the same about bears in the wild. There was never any glass between us and the bears, unfortunately.

As I stared out into the ocean, I heard a voice behind me. "Zach, where in tarnation have you been?"

I turned and gave Ellie an innocent grin. "I'm sorry. I ran off and then I got lost. But at least you found me."

She folded her arms in front of her. "Seriously? Do you have any sense of direction?"

"None whatsoever."

She sighed. "Have you seen Cor? We have a bit of a problem."

I frowned a little. "Yeah, we had an argument, and then went our separate ways."

"Seriously? Are the two of you daft? We're in a place that doesn't like Kausians, and you split up? Why are men such idiots?"

I gave her a shrug. "Because we are. Haven't you learned anything over the past few years?"

Ellie rolled her eyes. "Anyway, to the important topic. Gabe has been kidnapped, and we need to either find Cor and get our weapons or just go get our weapons and save him."

My eyes widened. "Wait, what? Kidnapped?"

She nodded. "Yup, saw it all myself—and saw where they took him. Hopefully they are those villains who reveal everything to the captor thinking they could never escape so we know exactly what is going on."

"Hopefully. That always helps. It's usually about a

seventy-five percent chance they do that."

"Right. Let's get back to our room, hope Cor is there, but either way, we need to grab some weapons in order to help Gabe."

I followed Ellie as she turned down the hallway. She turned two corners, and I realized how close I really was. Was it an improvement that I was getting closer to where I needed to go, or was it still bad that I couldn't find my way back when I was this nearby? Either way, it was definitely something I needed to work on and stop relying on Ellie.

Ellie opened the door and found that the room was quiet. There was no sign of Cor, which didn't surprise me. He probably went somewhere to be all angsty like he normally did.

"Damn it, Cor, where are you?" Ellie cursed under her breath.

I followed her to our room, and she pulled out our guns that we had brought with us and some of the tranks we purchased before we got on the ship down here.

"We'll need our guns for sure. I want to be in and out quickly without anyone noticing or coming as backup…"

"How do you think we can do this without being noticed?" I asked as I grabbed my gun Lucky Susan.

Ellie quickly changed into her old clothes. "Well, first we need to get into clothes with more mobility, and then we'll have to make our way through the air ducts."

I sighed. Why did it always have to be air ducts?

# CHAPTER XII

Gabe

Why did I keep finding myself in these predicaments? Seriously, it was getting annoying.

Who was even after me here? I would get a look at them once we arrived to wherever they were taking me —then I would know. Or at least I would see who actually grabbed me. And then, from there, I could figure out what was going on.

I had no idea how I was going to get out of this one. The others didn't know when I would be back, nor did they know anything about this place to find me. It wasn't as if they could ask around and get any info, as they were not from this place and no one knew them or trusted them. No, I was royally screwed.

We turned to the stairwell, and the men led me down the stairs. I tried to shove them and make them lose their footing in hopes they would let me go, but that only led to me almost falling. The guards were kind enough to stop me from doing that. I tried to be as loud as I could without completely screaming as I knew that would just lead to them beating me. I didn't want that. But if someone overheard some thrashing around, perhaps then they would come and help me. Maybe.

I was just glad they didn't abduct my sister as well. It was clear they only wanted me. If they wanted her, they would have grabbed us both at the same time. Whoever it was didn't want to harm her, so it was definitely not an attack against the country—just an attack against me.

At least my family would be all right. I hoped.

I wondered if they were going to go after Cor and the others. If that were the case, and they were able to escape or take down their attackers, then they would come for me. I hoped that was indeed true and someone knew where I had gone. Otherwise, this was going to be a long day.

It didn't seem like they wanted me dead, which was a good thing. They could have killed me already and dumped my body somewhere. Or perhaps someone specific wanted to do the honors. One couldn't rule that out.

Like my uncle.

We were now on the first floor. Since this place was my home, I could tell where these men were taking me. If I wasn't mistaken, we were nearing the guard's break room. That didn't bode well for wanting them to help us take down Byron—especially since he was probably the one who was behind this. Apparently he had all the military under his control.

I should have known it was a mistake coming here. I'd just thought I could count on my mother.

We took another turn, and yeah, we were definitely in the guard's break room. The men slammed me down into a chair and then tied my body to the chair. I didn't resist as I knew there was no point—they outnumbered me and I wasn't exactly the best at fighting with my fists. I made a mental note to work on that.

The hood came off, and I found half a dozen guards

in the room, glaring at me. Their eyes were all dark, and they watched me intently as if I were supposed to do something magnificent.

I smiled a little as I spotted one of the guards who was at the front gate. "And here I thought you didn't recognize me. Turns out you just didn't want to let on the fact that you did know me and were ordered to abduct me. Let me guess. Byron?"

The guard from earlier folded his arms in front of himself. "Perhaps. Or perhaps your people just don't want an outsider bringing even more outsiders to our home."

Which still was on par with Byron. He had gotten to them, or perhaps generations of being isolated from the world kept them like this. On top of Byron spitting poison wherever he goes.

"And then what? You going to kill me? Are you going to grab the others? What's your plan here?"

The men hesitated, which answered my question. I couldn't believe all of them were in on it. This was not going to end well. "So you are following Byron's orders, and he'll just deal with me when he gets here. Any idea when my loving uncle will be here?"

They looked at each other as if debating about saying

anything. Clearly they hadn't done this before, and they didn't know what to do with me. I wasn't sure if that was a good sign or bad sign. I let out a sigh. "I assume sooner rather than later. Are you capturing the others, or was this a plan he put in motion the moment I left?"

More glances. I laughed. "Seriously? You all can't answer a simple question. It's not as if I'm going to get some advantage knowing the truth. I'll just have an understanding why my own people would go out and betray their prince like this."

"Our prince?" One of the guards stood up and spat at my feet. He was tall—at least a foot taller than me. If I recalled correctly, he had been upstairs when I was searching for my mother. I was surprised he didn't just grab me right then and there. "As if any of us would call you our prince. You aren't one of us—you could never be one of us. You don't belong here and should have never been born."

I shook my head, the smile never leaving my lips. "You think I've never heard that one before? Do you think I was welcomed anywhere with open arms in my childhood? No. Do you think those words—those lies my uncle put in your head and everyone else's heads— matter? You're wrong."

They all stared at me as if surprised by what I had said. Did they think I would plead? Did they think saying they would never accept me would make me cry? I would be lying if I said they didn't hurt me a little, but overall, their words didn't affect me as much as they thought they would.

"Besides, why are you all taking orders from a human like that? Shouldn't you be thinking for yourself? Shouldn't you be figuring out how to solve your problems without outside help? Did you even hate me before he came in? Did you even know about me before he showed up and spread lies? I don't even want the throne—I don't want to be here. But Byron, he's done a lot of bad stuff. I wouldn't put it past him to double-cross you all and do something to my mother. Then what—how are you going to explain that to everyone? That you let a human in who killed the queen?"

I wanted to go on about what happened, but one of the guards grabbed a piece of cloth and gagged me with it. "That's enough out of you. We aren't listening to your lies. We don't trust half breeds—especially ones who associate with Kausians. We know Byron means well—he cares about our kingdom. Ever since his brother decided to have a child with our queen, he has been nothing but supportive in trying to get that relationship destroyed. We have every reason to trust him. He just wants every nation to mind their own business."

I shook my head and tried to tell them the truth, but it all came out as mumbles. It was no use anyway—they weren't going to listen. The tall guard from earlier put his fingers to his ears.

"Nah, nah, nah. I'm not listening to your rubbish. Your thoughts don't matter—you have no idea what he has done for our kind since you were born."

Oh, I had a feeling. It was probably something similar to what he lied about to Cor and to the Silurians before he stabbed them all in the back. And he was going to do the same to my people.

Even though everyone hated me, even though they wished I were never born, I wouldn't want this nation destroyed. One day they will understand that humans and Sirians and Lyrans and the other races were all the same. We were all living beings that mattered. I wouldn't deny them that future.

A few of them left the room to go back to their duty, and I glanced around, wondering if I could make an escape. There were still about three guards in here, which I doubted I could take out, especially since I was tied to this chair and had no weapons. Another note to self: learn how to get free while tied up.

That one I really should have known, but Cor always figured he would save me if I were in trouble and never bothered to teach me. Granted, I was a pain to teach anything to. I got distracted a lot and didn't pay attention if I wasn't interested. After everything that had happened, now, however, I was indeed interested.

As I sat there in the room for a bit, wondering what to do and how I was going to get out of this, I heard a loud thud coming from one of the walls. I turned my head to see what it was when suddenly the grate to the airshaft flew off the wall and Ellie and Zach appeared.

How in the world did they find me here?

The guards were quick to get up and reach for their guns but not as quick as Ellie and Zach were. Ellie shot two of them in the chest, and Zach got the last one in the leg. They went down like flies.

Ellie hurried over and took the gag out of my mouth.

"Did you just kill them all?" I knew I shouldn't care about the lives of the people who kidnapped me, but they were still my people. I didn't want them all to die just because they believed some psychopath's lies.

Ellie shook her head as she worked at the knots that tied me to the chair. "No, we used our tranks. We don't like killing people if we don't have to. Mainly because bullets are expensive."

I laughed. "Right. Well, let's get out of here before the others notice."

We opened the door to find there was no one in the hallway. I knew this wasn't normal and wondered if it had anything to do with them trying to kidnap me, they were looking for the Kausians, or if Byron was planning something else.

I didn't like it though. I didn't like it at all.

# CHAPTER XIII

Cor

I kicked the metal that was below the glass that made up the wall. I was still pissed off at Zach, mainly because I knew he was right. I didn't know what I wanted because I still felt so completely useless and guilty. It was their choice to stay with me, but should they? Was Zach right? Was I stringing them along to no real future?

I didn't deserve any of them. I didn't deserve the love Ellie still had for me, and I didn't deserve how much

Gabe trusted me after everything. I should leave right then and there and never show my face again.

No, that wasn't the answer. I always resorted to running away, and I knew this time it would end in disaster, not that the other times ended well either. The others needed me to help them take out Byron. I wanted to kill him and would stop at nothing to succeed. He had destroyed my life and everything I had loved. He used me to get the codes for the shield that went around Kaus, knowing my parents were in charge of that. Not many people knew the codes, but I had memorized them when I was little, just in case something happened.

And something did happen. All because of me.

I was forced to tell Byron and Krax what the codes were. Krax probably thought they were a team. But then Byron used Krax to start a new war against the Silurians. I wondered how far that had developed and whether their zone had been destroyed like Kaus. It would take some time for the nations to really turn on the Silurians, however. Something like that didn't just happen overnight.

But I had a feeling there were a lot of pub fights in the Lyran and Human Zones. The Silurians would be driven out of the two zones and forced to hide, just like the Kausians had for over a century or so. The tricky thing about the Silurians was that they were a little more advanced when it came to technology, and going to war with them could cause them to destroy someone else. It was probably a standstill at this point.

Did I really care? Not particularly since the Silurians were the ones who launched the attack on my people even if it had been Byron who was pulling the strings. They both deserved to have their lives taken away from them. I didn't pity Krax for how he was killed—it was just that I didn't get to do it myself.

I let out a laugh. Perhaps I really didn't have room for love or compassion in my heart. I knew I didn't have the capability of forgiveness, which everyone says is a sign of compassion. Even if Byron repented, I could never forgive him and wanted to watch him suffer. He took everything away from me, and I would pay it all back tenfold.

But how would I do that? He didn't seem to care about family like Krax did. The only thing he cared about was destroying the world. It wasn't easy to make someone like that miserable other than by stopping their plans. But that didn't seem vengeful enough for me. I needed something else to stop this sorrowful feeling I had in my chest.

Taking a deep breath, I let it out slowly. First I needed to focus and get this all figured out. We would get Gabe's mom to help us, we would go after Byron, and we would win this war. We had to or else the entire world would be destroyed. Or at least everyone but the humans would be destroyed.

I tapped my fist lightly on the glass, then turned on my heel and headed to the room. Zach and Ellie should be back by now, and we needed to figure out what to do next. Then, once Gabe was back, we could move forward. Hopefully he will have convinced his mom to listen and to lead a force against Byron. And if not, well, we would have to convince her of what happened.

If that was even possible.

I made it to the room to find it completely empty. I sighed as I checked the clock. It had been over an hour since Ellie and I had left to search for Zach, and we promised we would meet here. Perhaps she went looking for me since I didn't come back? Although she was as impatient as I was, she knew I probably just didn't want to come back due to Zach and me fighting. No, they must have left for a different reason.

Perhaps it had something to do with the two guards who had just jumped out from behind the couch at me.

I spun on my heel and deflected their advances. The joke was on them. I was used to surprise attacks and not just because of the past three years. No, it was because since we were little, Ellie liked to jump out and attack me whenever she had the chance. It was cute, as she never held back, and it usually ended up with her face falling in some mud. She always got Zach though. He never seemed to learn.

One of the men pulled out a trank gun, but not before I grabbed a beautiful, ornate piece of glass and smashed it over his head. He went down like a sack of potatoes. The second guard pulled out his actual gun, but I was faster. I grabbed the first guard's Taser and jammed it into the second guard's side. He went down, twitching. Knowing I couldn't keep him conscious, I smacked a nice vase over his head.

Well, it was apparent that Ellie and Zach were probably kidnapped and I had to go save their butts. Yippee.

I didn't know this place very well, so they could have been anywhere. I needed Gabe to help me, but I also didn't know where he was. Did I wait for him, possibly giving the bad guys some time to torture or kill Zach and Ellie if they weren't already dead? Or did I wait for him and have a better chance of finding them? Decisions, decisions.

Opening the door, I found three figures in the hallway. I pointed my gun at them as Ellie pulled out her gun at me. We both stared at each other for a moment.

She sighed. "You really want to be shot, don't you?"

I raised an eyebrow. "I just knocked two guards out and was going to go save you guys, so how about you say thank you instead of trying to shoot me?"

"So they came after you too? That's not good," Gabe commented as he stepped into his room. "Oh no, what did you do the sculpture I made when I was twelve?"

I glanced down at the broken glass. "I, uh, am sorry? It was the closest thing I could find. If I had known…"

"It's all right. Don't worry about it. I'd rather you be all right."

I smiled and gave him a quick kiss. I didn't turn to Ellie or Zach as I knew they were both shooting daggers at me with their eyes. "So, tell me, what did your mother say?"

Gabe's smile disappeared. "I didn't find her. I did,

however, get kidnapped, and these two here saved me just now."

My jaw opened a little. "Wait, what? They caught you?" I turned to Ellie and Zach. "How did you two manage to save him?"

"Well," Ellie began. "While someone was out being angsty, I saw them kidnap Gabe and followed to where they were holding him. Then I made my way back and ran into Zach, luckily. Then we grabbed our weapons and went to take them out. We did just that, and now we're here."

That was a lot to take in. "Who was behind it? Was it Byron?"

Gabe nodded. "Yup. It seems since, well, forever, my uncle decided to turn the people against me, and they've been waiting until I returned. I presume they alerted him the moment we arrived and he is on his way."

I rubbed my forehead. This was all just dandy. "Does your mother know about this? I mean, she has to, right? She's the queen."

He shrugged. "Beats me. I doubt it though. She was always oblivious when he was out to get me as a child. I had hoped things had changed, but clearly they hadn't.

Besides, she wouldn't let someone hurt me, that much I know. She was strangely protective and blind to what was going on at the same time. She was good at tracking me on Mu, which was annoying and always led to Byron finding me since she would tell my father where I was." Gabe bit at his thumbnail. "I always have wondered how much he has known about this, although I really hope he isn't involved. I haven't seen him for years. I'm sorry for dragging you all here for nothing. I'm afraid we really fucked up coming down here."

Ellie shook her head. "No, you haven't talked to your mom. We can still make this happen. We just have to go and tell her what's going on, and maybe she can stop it —maybe she can convince the people of what's really happening."

Gabe let out a defeated sigh. "I suppose it's worth a shot. I'm just afraid that perhaps they don't... I'm worried her people might turn on her."

All of us stared at him. I was the first to ask the obvious question. "What makes you say that?"

"Just the way the guards were acting, not to mention the fact they aren't stationed where they normally are. I mean, there never were that many guards around usually, but something still seems off. I think they're planning something when he gets here, and I'm worried. I mean, I presume a lot of them are still on her side, but I just don't know. I don't like how the guards were completely on Byron's side. He has brainwashed them, just like he brainwashes everyone."

He had a point there. I would know—he did that to me. I paced back and forth in the room, careful not to trip over the two guards.

"I think first thing's first—we need to go to your mother and try to convince her. I don't think she'll listen if all of us are there. I'll go with you and make sure none of the guards try to get you again. Ellie and Zach, I want you to circle around and see if you can figure out when Byron is coming." I glanced down at the bodies. "And I have the perfect idea of how you are going to do that."

# CHAPTER XIV

Ellie

#

I couldn't believe we were doing this.

We could be arrested if not killed on the spot. Then again, it seemed like the entire world was out to get us anyway, so this was our best option. I fidgeted in the guard clothes we had stolen off those men and sighed.

I tugged on the brown, fish scale-like tunic, trying to straighten it. "They're going to kill us for shifting, you know that right?"

Zach shrugged. "They're going to kill us anyway.

Might as well do this. Besides, you could have said something about the plan to Cor, but you didn't want to disagree with him, did you?"

I rolled my eyes. "What is up with you today? Are you really that mad at him?"

He shrugged again. "I just don't like how he's playing both you and Gabe, that's all."

I shook my head. "No, that isn't all of it. I mean, I know he's going through things, and so am I. There are a lot of emotions we're still figuring out. I don't know what to do, Zach. He was the love of my life, and we were going to spend the rest of our lives together. Then everything that happened… but then finding out all the secrets had to do with wanting to make a better life for me… I just don't know."

Zach frowned a little. "You two were very close. You always had been. But he still left us."

"I know. And it hurt. But I guess I understand why he did it after hearing his story. I mean, it was still a stupid idea, but we were young and traumatized. It wasn't just a place that was destroyed. It was everyone we knew. Gone. In an instant. I would have run too if I were in his shoes."

Zach was quiet for a moment. I had a feeling he

agreed. So much had happened in such a short amount of time. It took us a long while to process it all. I was in shock for at least two or three days before it hit me. Our home and family were gone. And there was nothing we could do to get it back.

"Where would you two have gone?" Zach finally asked.

I glanced at him and for a moment forgot that we were transformed into the two guards who had tried to kidnap Cor. I turned forward, acting like I was a guard on duty. "What do you mean?"

"I mean, if Cor was able to go to some human university, get a nice job, would you have left Kaus and stayed in some other zone? Would you have left everything behind like that?"

Now I realized what this was about. It didn't have anything to do with him not liking Cor or about how Gabe was now involved with this. No, it had to do with him thinking we were going to leave him behind when we moved forward with our lives.

"Zach... we wouldn't have left you. I would never have left you. You could have come with. We would have found a place for the three of us. My future was never going to be without you, okay? It still isn't. If after all this was done and Cor and I ended up together, you would be there too. You are my best friend and mean as much to me as he does. I love you, Zach. It's just a different love than what I have for Cor. It doesn't mean I love Cor more. It just means I want to be with him differently."

It was strange to watch Zach's expressions as he was transformed into one of the Sirian guards. He wiped away a tear from his eye. "That means a lot, Ellie. I love you too. I just don't want to be left alone. Not again."

I gave him a tight hug. "And I wouldn't let that happen. Who else is going to have my back? And help check the bathrooms for guys trying to kill us? And provide for our horses? And I ain't trusting Cor to clean my gun for me. He'd probably never give it back since it's such a nice gun."

"It is. It really is."

"And you know better than to steal from me."

"I do. I really do."

I stepped back. "Now come on, we have a mission to complete. We have to figure out if Byron is indeed coming and whether he has a plan in motion to destroy the Sirian Zone like he's trying to do to the Silurian

Zone."

Zach nodded. "Right. I would assume he is since he wants to take out every other race so no mixed breeding happens."

"That would make sense, but would he really start two wars at once? Or would he try something else? If I were him, I wouldn't start two wars at once—otherwise the Lyran would realize what was going on and team up. No, whatever he's going to try to do here is going to be a bit different."

"What do you think he has in mind?"

I shrugged. "Not sure, but we have to figure out what it is before it's too late."

We ventured down the corridors, careful not to cause attention. I knew that people were starting to arrive, as there were a few when we went to save Gabe. They were all being escorted up the stairs toward the banquet hall that was on the second level. We ventured down the stairs to take a look to see how large this event was going to be.

I expected the banquet to be a lie, as I didn't think someone could put together such a big event on such short notice. Apparently I was wrong and these people did it all the time. I tried not to stare at the fancy robes of all different types, each a rainbow of astonishing colors. One woman wore a robe that was the same color as the sea with fish dyed into the fabric. One man had a black robe that was adorned with stars and on the back was the moon. If it weren't for the fact that we were on a mission, I would stare at them for even longer.

But we couldn't be spotted—not with our eyes.

So we kept our heads down, careful not to make any direct eye contact. Hopefully we wouldn't get called out by any high-ranking person, otherwise they would notice we weren't looking them in the eye. Although, depending on the person, they might not notice and think we were doing it because we were below them. Maybe that would actually work in our favor.

We made our way through the crowd and to the other end of the second floor. So far, we hadn't raised any suspicion, but we also hadn't found any clues or spotted anyone who wasn't Sirian. Byron wasn't hiding on that level. At least not that I could tell.

"Where do you think we should look now?" I asked.

Zach glanced around. "I think most of the clues would be in the guard's break room, but they will more than likely notice us there."

"Or, at least, they will notice our eyes. They will be

searching for us since we escaped with Gabe and because those two guards they sent to Gabe's room never came back. We look identical to them now. Odds are, they might not notice if we don't look at them in the eye."

"But what do we say about why we, or they, failed the mission?"

"We just say they escaped and are on the loose. I mean, that's what happened to the ones who were watching Gabe."

"Wouldn't that make things harder for Gabe and Cor?"

I shrugged. "They are already on the lookout for all of us. I think it will be the best thing to say if we do get questioned."

"Well then, I guess we should try there. Lead the way, because frankly, I don't remember where it was."

I chuckled as I turned toward the stairs. Hopefully this wouldn't end up as horribly as I imagined it would.

# CHAPTER XV

Zach

Would this end horribly? Or would it work?

If history repeated itself, which it typically did, this all would wind up badly, but in the end, we would miraculously get away or make some big breakthrough and solve our problems but not without some cuts and bruises. I hoped it would go a bit better than that, as I hated having cuts and bruises, but I just wanted to stop whatever awful thing was about to happen. If I were honest with myself, I felt bad for what had happened up on Zynon and partially responsible.

Granted, the Silurians weren't that great of a race and had caused us more trouble than any other species, not to mention they were the ones who led the attack against Kaus. The men could have resisted—they could have questioned why their leader was giving them orders to kill all the people in the casino, but they didn't. They seemed to care very little about the lives of others. But that didn't mean I wasn't somewhat guilty. Byron had forced me to transform into their leader and give the orders—threatening me with my life. I knew that Ellie would make it through it all—she always did —not to mention she knew Byron was up to something that night and stayed alert. I saw how quickly she and Cor got under the tables. They were used to a shoot-out after all the years of people after them. After us.

None of this was fair.

I prayed to the goddess that years from now, whether we were still alive or not, that all the nations could live in harmony, but I knew that future was looking bleak. Even if the race issue wasn't a problem, there was still the problem of class, and I didn't know how that was going to change. I just wanted to find a cottage somewhere with my friends and forget everyone else existed. That was originally Ellie's and my plan, until some outlaws found us and tried to take it away. That was when the bounty hunting started as we took the men in for the reward. Well, that and a few other things that happened, which was how we'd gotten our horses. That was a long story for another day though.

Ellie led us down different hallways and stairs, and I felt even more turned around. My next goal in life was to have a better sense of direction. But for now, I would rely on Ellie to get us there.

There were fewer people on the first level, as many of the guests were already up on the second level where the banquet was. I was surprised by how many Sirians were showing up to the shindig for Gabe's return, though I had a feeling it was more of a social thing than actually welcoming him back. These people didn't seem to like him. It was one thing to be at a normal level in society and everyone hate you. It was a completely different thing to be their leader's son and have the entire nation despise you.

The guards were scattered throughout the second and first floor, making sure the guests were safe and more than likely looking for us. We moved past them, as if we had to be somewhere due to some orders. No one questioned us but kept on doing what they too were ordered to do.

We made our way through the first floor. The hallways were very mazelike, which always had me turned around. At least the first few floors had a large middle stairwell that opened up, taking away some of the square footage, and with it the mazelike hallway compared to the higher levels. It didn't mean I could find what we were looking for, however. There was still a lot of space to get lost in.

As we came up on a hallway that appeared similar, I felt a little proud of myself for remembering which air duct we had snuck into. Mainly because it was still open, but I was still a bit proud. Ellie nodded to the door up ahead, and I slowly opened it.

To both of our surprise, there were no guards in the break room. More than likely, since the banquet was about to start, they were all on duty. Or perhaps the ones who were supposed to be off duty were the two we were disguised as. Either way, we were in the clear.

Ellie closed the door behind her. "Okay, you search around for clues on that side, and I'll search on the other side."

I nodded. It seemed to be the most logical step. I

began to flip through papers that were out and about. Most of them were crosswords and word searches and fun little games like that. I skimmed through the newspapers they had, catching up on any politics that were being reported. One of the articles talked about what happened up on Zynon.

"Oh, Ellie," I commented. "You have to look at this."

Ellie came over and looked through the article. "Seriously? Everyone is buying that Krax was the one who started the shoot-out and that Byron saved the day?"

"Yup."

"I mean, he was pretty convincing, but we know the truth."

"We do. Do you think we'll be able to convince anyone else of the truth though? I mean, everyone loves him. Well, everyone but the Silurians…"

She pointed at the end of the article. "It seems the rest of the Silurian government is trying to make some kind of peace treaty with the other nations, promising it will never happen again. They're even pulling all Silurians from other nations."

"Interesting. I would have assumed they would have gone for more of an aggressive approach."

Ellie shrugged. "Well, I mean, it could be an act. They need some time to come up with a little strategy. Also, since Krax is dead, they need to figure out a new leader. That can't be easy."

She had a point there. If I recalled correctly, there was a whole tournament for the next leader that lasted at least a week, even longer depending on who was telling the story. I flipped through the rest of the paper. "Well, besides that, I don't see any other clues in this paper."

"I mean, they aren't going to announce treason or whatever in a paper…," Ellie said, smugly.

I put the paper down. "You knew what I meant! I thought maybe some other civil unrest could be in it. Usually when people want to take down a prince, there is something else going on."

"We already know why they want to do it—they don't like half-humans and Byron made that even worse."

"I guess. It just seems odd they would be so quick to do something."

"Byron must have some backup plans in place for all of us. I don't think it matters where we go; he will have someone ready. That's what happens when you have way too much money on your hands."

I nodded. That was for sure. I wondered how many bounty hunters he had sent after Gabe and how many Cor took out. "It's crazy to think that we were sent to kill Gabe, and here we are now, trying to figure all this out. I'm glad we stopped and listened to him."

"It was only because he knew Cor though. If he hadn't known Cor, his blood would be on our hands."

We were both quiet for a moment. Now it was making me wonder how many innocent lives we had taken. I knew most of the men we went after were bad. There were bounties on all their heads for killing or assaulting one person or another. Or from robbing a bank. But Gabe was one of the few, if not the only person, who didn't have a record that we took on—all because we were looking for Cor.

"What do you think we will do after all this is over? As a job, I mean?"

She shrugged. "Well, hopefully Gabe lives and still has access to his family's bank account. If that's the case, I think we'll be set."

I laughed. "That's true. If he wants anything to do with us."

"That's fair."

It all depended on Cor and Ellie, really. I liked Gabe and would love to stay as friends. I felt I could connect with him. But the three of them were in some weird, awkward love triangle, so I would just have to sit on the sidelines and watch it explode. I did not look forward to that.

Silence filled the room once more. I kept searching for anything I could find on what their plan was, but all I found was some more games, one involving numbers, some disgusting porn books, and old new papers. I decided any notes on their plan were definitely not on my side of the room.

"Ah, bingo!" Ellie called over from her side of the room.

I rushed to find that she had a paper with some notes written on it.

Ellie shook her head in disbelief. "This has got to be the most simplistic plan ever. He must have made it like this so these guys would remember. If Gabe is right, they probably have had this plan ready for a while."

I looked over the paper. It literally had four numbered points on it that read:

1. Kidnap Gabriel Pickett
2. Alert Byron

3. Keep Him Alive

4. Deliver Gabriel To Byron

"Yeah, that's pretty simple, Ellie. Then again, Byron's directions were simple for us. He must not like to complicate things for fear that whoever he has hired will mess them up."

"Makes sense to me. Keep it simple, stupid."

I turned to her. "But do you think that's the only plan he has going on? I mean, he may make things simple for the people he hires, but he himself has a very complicated system of plans going on at once."

She nodded. "You're right. He probably has some other stuff going on that these guards don't know about. My guess is that he was alerted when we arrived and will probably get here, well, around now. So he is more than likely going to do something with the banquet tonight. Whether it's a shoot-out like last time or something as equally sinister, we'll have to stop it before it's too late."

"Right. Let's go scope around."

# CHAPTER XVI

Gabe

This would totally go according to plan. It had to. Otherwise, I was probably a dead man and my entire home would be destroyed.

I took some deep, calming breaths and tried to think of it all rationally. My mother would listen to me. I would save everyone. I would be regarded as a hero.

Okay, probably not that last bit, but maybe they would grow to accept me. It wasn't my drive though or at least not my main drive. Everyone wanted a place to belong, and perhaps after all this was over, I finally would have a place I could feel at home.

Cor followed me, keeping an eye out for any guards who were looking for us. I wanted to say it felt strange being on the lookout for someone wanting to hurt me in my own home, but it actually felt more natural than anything. Byron liked to make people hate me—it was his favorite pastime. So I constantly had people bullying me and locking me in some closet for a few hours or so overnight.

At least this time I knew there was someone out there who wanted to help me.

But now I was older and wiser and knew I had some self-worth. Now I knew that I could try to protect myself and my friends by talking face-to-face with my mother and making her see the truth. It wouldn't change my past, but I was not going to let it stop my future. No, I would make things right once and for all.

"Turn right up ahead," I said. "Last my sister saw her, she was in the kitchen, getting everything ready."

"Sister?" Cor asked. "You have a sister?"

Right. I forgot to mention that. "Yeah. She's my half-sister and is about five or six now. She was still really little when I left, and I didn't get to spend much time with her. I didn't even think she knew I existed until I ran into her."

"So I take it she's the heir to all this."

"Bingo. No way the likes of me would ever become ruler. I don't want it anyway. Can you imagine me ruling all the Sirians?"

He chuckled. "Not really."

I stuck my tongue out at him. "You were supposed to say that I could do anything I could set my mind to."

"Yeah, but you just said that you didn't want to be the ruler. You wouldn't want to be stuck to one place, would you? You seem like you would want to travel the world and see what it's all about. Being stuck down here doesn't suit you. Maybe a diplomat to different zones but not a king."

He had a point there, but was it that I wanted to travel, or was it the fact that I was trying to find somewhere that I could call home? Those thoughts ate at me as we made it to the kitchen.

I entered to find that my mother had already left. There were about a dozen chefs all scrambling around the room, trying to prepare smoked halibut, steamed prawns, sautéed shrimp, seaweed salads, and whatever ingenious creations they had in store. Although I had a feeling I wasn't going to get to enjoy the banquet, I hoped I got to at least try some of the food. If it weren't for the fact I really needed to talk to my mother, I would have stayed there and made sure everything was up to par.

Some of the chefs were young, as if they were interns who had just been hired. I didn't recognize them, but some of the older chefs I did recognize. Although many of the guards picked on me, all the cooks were always kind and made me some special desserts every once in a while to cheer me up. They didn't really talk to me, but I knew even then what they were trying to do, and I appreciated it.

I stepped up to one of the men who was making rice rolls. "Do you know where the queen went off to? I was told she was in here."

He turned to me and bowed his head a little. "She went back to her room to prepare, my prince."

I nodded a thank-you. It seemed he remembered who I was. That made me feel a bit special, as I had lost hope for anyone in this palace caring about me after what happened to me after my run-in with the guards. Then again, perhaps this was a front, and the chefs were going to alert the guards to where I was the moment I turned my back. Hopefully that was not the case, but years in this place had made me paranoid.

"Thank you. I'm looking forward to tonight's feast. I'm sure it is going to be wonderful. Just as always."

He bowed again. "Thank you, my prince. You are too kind."

I spun on my heel, and Cor and I turned to head to my mother's room, which was, of course, near the top of the palace. We had at least twelve flights of stairs to climb.

"Hasn't your kind heard of elevators?" Cor huffed as we ventured up and up.

I shrugged. "I think they tried it once and it didn't work with the humidity here. There are passages in which you can swim up and down, but then you end up wet. This castle has only twenty flights and is how we all stay in shape."

"It would seem like you would have to. What about those who can't walk though? Like the elderly and whatnot."

"If they are coming to the palace, they more than likely have hired some people to carry them in a palanquin. I'm surprised we haven't seen many yet."

"You rich people making others do all the work."

I laughed as we went up the stairs. I had to admit, my legs were getting quite sore after all this walking and climbing up and down the palace. When I woke up tomorrow, I was not going to be able to move. Hopefully I could still run away if need be.

After much huffing and puffing, we arrived at the level my mother's room was on. We quietly made our way down the corridor, and Cor kept his gun out, ready to shoot any guard we came across. Even if it weren't all the guards who were in on this, we didn't want to be too careful. Besides, he was using tranks and wasn't going to actually kill them.

Cor peered around the corner and turned back to me.

"There are four of them outside a room with giant doors. I presume it's your mother's room?"

I nodded. "Yeah, all the rooms she usually is in have huge doors. Not sure why. It's not like royalty are taller than normal folk."

Cor shook his head with a slight laugh. "That was completely something Zach would say. You know that, right?"

I had been joking, but I had to agree, it was something Zach would say. Whether he was serious or not would be a completely different story.

Cor made sure he had enough tranks in his gun and then stepped around the corner. I heard his gun fire four times and then the thud of a guard collapsing with each and every shot.

I stepped out from behind the corner and gave Cor a hug and a kiss. "My hero."

He blushed a little, and what I had said made him smile. "Come on, we don't have all day."

I unwrapped my arms and started toward the door to my mother's room. "How many tranks do you have left?" I asked as I glanced down at the bodies.

"Enough," he said. "And you have your gun, you know. Once in a while, you should try shooting these guys."

I pulled it out and examined it. "It just feels so weird —I keep thinking I'm going to kill them."

"Don't worry. I haven't given you any real bullets. Your guns only have tranks."

I frowned. "But what if I miss? Then I'll have wasted them. You know I'm not a great shot."

"That's okay. They're cheaper. And you have money apparently." He raised an eyebrow at me.

I knew I should have told him the truth of who I was a long while ago, but I could never find the right moment to tell him. Then the longer I waited, the worse I felt until the truth was revealed by Byron.

"Hey, if I used my card, then my mother would tell Byron where we were. I had to be careful. We had to make our own money. I only used it when she figured out where I was."

"Mm-hmm." He reloaded his gun and put it away. "You realized you could have withdrawn a bunch of cash and then we could have just run for it, right?"

I shrugged. "Then you would have asked how I got all that money, and I would have had to tell you the truth."

"Whatever," he commented as he turned to the door. "So, are you ready?"

"No, but I have to do it. Are you sure you'll be fine out here alone?"

"I have to keep you safe somehow." He kissed me on the lips. "Besides, she won't listen to you if I'm there. Now, tell her what happened and we can finally get all this behind us."

I nodded and reached for the door handle. This was my only chance to convince her of what was going on. Otherwise, the entire world as we knew it would be destroyed.

# CHAPTER XVII

Gabe

I opened the door to find two servants doing my mother's makeup. Truth be told, she didn't need it—she was as beautiful as the moon itself. But it was customary for women to wear makeup, and so she plastered her face with white foundation and colorful eye shadow every morning and every evening even if there were no guests in the palace, just in case. I had a feeling after I left my sister, someone came and applied her makeup as well. I was glad men only rarely had to wear makeup, as it always made my face itch.

She was wearing her evening robe as she got her face and hair ready and would eventually put on her dress that she had picked out for the evening. I had a feeling it would be colorful, mesmerizing, and stand out from all the rest of the guests, especially since no one had time to get something special made for the occasion. For a lot of these events, men and women would have something specially made and to never be worn again. It was a waste of clothes if you asked me, but my mother always had so many sets of clothes that she had yet to wear so she could put on last-minute events like these. Whether it was because she liked to be prepared herself and declare an event on the spot just to frustrate the guests about not having an outfit to wear was beyond me.

My mother's suite was larger than my own, but it was not divided into three rooms. Instead, there was a large sitting area on the left, her makeup and dressing area beyond that, then her bed was on the right. She also had a large walk-in closet that was almost as big as my guest room, and her bathroom was practically a spa. Before she became queen, this room was my grandmother's and her mother's before that. It was passed down to whoever was queen. I assumed before my mother was queen, she had a room similar to my own.

Glancing up at me from the mirror, my mother furrowed her eyebrows that were now painted up higher on her forehead. "Riri, what are you doing here? Why are you not dressed?"

I glanced down. I was back in my human clothes as they were a lot easier to run in. Also, they wouldn't stand out if we had to go back to shore. Just in case. "I need to speak with you. Alone."

She did not like that I was asking the servants to leave when she needed to get ready. Guests had already arrived, and although it was customary for royalty to enter later than everyone, she still had to put on her dress. I, however, could help her with that.

My mother pursed her lips, then nodded to the servants. The two women bowed and left my mother and me to talk. One obstacle was out of the way, now I just needed to get my mother to listen to me.

I stood there, silent, not sure how to start this conversation. I wanted more than anything to just spill everything. I wanted to tell her all the things Byron had said to me over the years, the lies he had spread about me, what he had done to Cor, and how he orchestrated everything that had happened on Zynon. But would that be too much for her to handle? I knew if I started to talk, I wouldn't stop, and I needed to figure out a way to keep this brief so she could go down and try to raise an army before it was too late.

Not sure what to do about my silence, my mother stood up and walked over to her couch. "Come sit next to me and tell me what's the matter. Is it those Kausians? Did they do something to hurt you?"

Well, technically Ellie and Zach did try to kill me, but that was before everything and not the point. I sat down next to her and took in her scent, fearing it would be the last time I got to smell it.

Gathering all the strength I had, I told her the truth. "Mother, Uncle Byron is trying to turn the nations against each other and destroy one another so that humans will rule Mu."

She stared at me for a moment, then shook her head. "What are you talking about? He has been a diplomat for a long time—he just wants peace."

"No, you have no idea how vile he is. He tried to kill me multiple times. He sent bounty hunters after me, and up in Zynon, he was the one who made the Silurians kill all those people—not Krax."

She shook her head. "That's not possible. Your uncle would never—"

"He did, Mother. I saw it with my own two eyes. He tried to have me killed up there in the process, but luckily I was wearing a bulletproof vest since I knew he wanted me dead. It was sheer luck that someone didn't shoot me in the head though."

My mother's mouth opened, then closed. I saw her clench her fist as she stood up and started pacing. "He has always been helpful to us Sirians. I can't believe he would try to start a war like that."

"It isn't the only war he started either. He was the one who convinced everyone that the Kausians were evil and going to attack us all. None of that was true. He then tricked Cor, one of the Kausians, into thinking he was going to put him through a university, only to force him to reveal the codes so that they could get in and attack. The Kausians were completely defenseless when Krax and his men bombed it. It was genocide, and Byron was behind it all."

My mother's eyes were tearing up. She went over and grabbed some tissues and dabbed her eyes, careful not to mess up her makeup. "Does your father know about this?"

I shook my head. "I don't know how much he knows or if he's simply keeping his head in the sand for it all, but I know that Byron is a very, very bad man and has made my life miserable because I'm half-human. He doesn't think any of the races should intermingle. He wants humans to be pure-blooded because he believes they are the strongest race."

Mother turned to peer out the glass. A gray shark swam by, startling me for a moment. My mother didn't even flinch. "He always said that he admired the Sirians because we were strong and held on to our beliefs. Perhaps that wasn't why he liked us—perhaps he liked us because we stay isolated and typically don't mingle with other races, especially down here. I wanted to change that—I wanted to learn from other races and welcome them with open arms. I hoped that with you I could change people's minds. It was all for nothing, wasn't it? I made you suffer in the process."

"No, you stood up for what you believed in, and I'm proud to call you my mother. It isn't your fault that people don't listen to you. But right now you have to listen to me. You have to arrest Byron if he is here. I think he might be coming for me, and I don't know exactly what he has planned for all of us. All I know is that he has the guards on his side." I hesitated, not sure if I should tell her what happened earlier. I knew she needed to know everything, however. "Earlier the guards kidnapped me so that Byron could come and get me. We can't trust them, and that is why I'm dressed how I am—in case I need to fight. We must find others to help us before it's too late. You must tell them what actually happened up in Zynon."

She bit at her nail—a habit I had picked up from her. "There are many diplomats here tonight, even on short notice. I'll tell them all the truth, and we can see who is on our side. The guards won't try anything against me —they know the people would riot. As for you, however—you'll need to hide until all this is finished. I will not let them get to you."

"Cor can keep me safe. I'll stay here until the night is over. Then we can begin putting together a plan of attack in the morning with those who wish to fight with us."

My mother patted away some of her tears. "I'm glad you came back and trusted me with this information, Riri. Together perhaps all my dreams will come true and we will be able to live in harmony with the other races."

I smiled, but after being on the outside for as long as I had, I knew that it would take much more work than that. I knew how deep the hatred went in many people's hearts. It would take a lot of time and effort. But if that hatred only took a few seeds that some had planted long ago, perhaps they could be run down with new seeds of hope and kindness.

"Now, I better fix my makeup and get my robe on. I wouldn't want anyone to know I was crying. A leader can't show weakness, Riri. Remember that."

I saw my mother in a new light. She truly wanted to stand up for what she believed in even if the entire nation didn't agree. She wanted peace more than anything. I wished I could have seen her and my father when they were younger and in love. It must have been so strong.

"I'll remember that, Mother."

# CHAPTER XVIII

Cor

I should have had Gabe help me with these bodies before he went into his mother's room. Now I had to throw them in some random closet all by myself.

And they were heavy. They seemed heavier than humans, something I had noticed in all my times in bed with them. It was ever so slight but noticeable enough when I moved them. Perhaps it was because they were similar to fish when it came to swimming even if that physical change wasn't present when they were dry.

I should have noticed Gabe was a little bit heavier than a human, but he was also a bit thin, so he already weighed less than me. He was also half, so that must have played a role in how his body was made up.

As I disposed of the last body and jimmied the door handle so it was hard to open and it would take them a bit to figure out, the door to the queen's chambers opened. I quickly hid behind one of the vases that was larger than me and watched as two servants left. Apparently the queen was willing to listen to Gabe. That was a good sign.

I watched them as they left, curious if they would go and alert guards that Gabe was speaking to his mother. If I were honest, I doubted they were a part of anything. Typically it was stupid guards who could get their minds poisoned with grandeur compared to servants or women. Women were smarter, and their hearts weren't turned as quickly as men's were. At least that was what it seemed like to me.

Unless you, of course, betray your kind by giving away the codes to your zone, leading to the destruction of everything.

Then hearts could turn, and the one person who you loved most—that loved you the most—would want you dead. I was surprised she didn't kill me right then and there for what happened. Instead, she listened to my story and believed I wasn't at fault.

But I was at fault—I had trusted the wrong person.

No matter what anyone said—no matter how many times I heard it—I couldn't forgive myself for what I had done. I could have let them kill me. I could have resisted and made a break for it. There would have been a way for me to get back and tell the others and save Ellie, the one person he said he would destroy if I didn't tell him right then and there. He was bluffing. I found out later he didn't have her hidden somewhere. No, I believe him and I gave them the codes like a scared little kid.

Because that was what I was—a scared little kid.

At the time anyway. I had thought I was smarter and different from the rest, but history indicated that wasn't the case. I didn't know how to put others before myself, and I didn't know how to ask for help. All I knew was that I was being given the chance to stand out, and I didn't even hesitate. I believed I was made for school and higher class, and he acted as if he agreed. He even spent a couple of months teaching me and gaining my trust so that I would be more likely to think he wouldn't do such horrible things with the codes as he did. Or perhaps he kept me around for a while just to play silly mind games and completely break my soul.

I should have known better—I should have known what they were going to do with the codes. I should have known it would end in blood—blood that was all on my hands.

I would get my revenge on Byron and then…

Well, I didn't know what to do then. It wouldn't bring my people back—it wouldn't change what happened. That didn't deter me from wanting to kill him, but it didn't exactly solve anything. It did stop other zones from being destroyed, but what did they ever do for my kind? Nothing. They just sat back and watched. I wasn't doing any of this for them. No, I was doing it for myself and for all the friends and family who died that day.

I was doing it for the life that was taken away from me.

Pacing outside the queen's room, I wondered how long it was going to take Gabe. Was the light bulb going to click for the queen and she would understand everything that had been going on was orchestrated by Byron? Or was she going to keep her head in the sand just like everyone else? I felt it could go either way and prayed that Gabe's mom had common sense to help us.

However, she didn't because we were Kausians. That wasn't a good sign as it meant she believed the filth that was given to her. She didn't ask our names or what we were doing with her son but assumed we were feeding him lies and there to take over or something. After hearing what many others believed we would do, I couldn't blame her. I just wished there was some place we could go where people would welcome us with open arms.

But perhaps Gabe could persuade her about Byron. Perhaps she would realize what he was up to. She had to help us—or we would be up shit creek.

There would be no one backing us up, and Byron had too many pieces into play for us to just kill him and walk away. For all we knew, he might have a plan in motion that with his death would just escalate things even further. We had to convince everyone what he was up to so they knew what to do to make it all right again —so they could stop another genocide.

I heard something fall from around the corner. I quickly pulled out my gun and stayed silent for a moment to see if I could hear anything else. There was silence. I slowly crept down the corridor, careful to not make any sound. So far, I didn't hear anything else. It was probably my imagination. It was probably just a mouse or a crab or something.

Rounding the corner, I found one of the marble decorations on the ground. It must have simply fallen off the pedestal. It was nothing to be alarmed about.

As I was about to turn back, I heard a click of a gun behind my head. I cursed under my breath. Apparently I was still too wrapped up in my head that I didn't think to check the other side of the hallway. Even so, there weren't many people who could do that, and after seeing how noisy the guards typically were, I knew it could only be one person.

"Byron."

He moved a little so I could see him. "Cornelius Adams. You must be quite distracted. Usually you aren't so easy to sneak up on."

I shrugged. "I guess my mind was elsewhere. And I didn't think you specifically would be down here in the Sirian Zone. I was more on the lookout for guards who were noisy and not so sly."

He laughed. "Well, I definitely have learned to be quiet and attack from the shadows. I'm sure after all the time you spent hunting down people, you have learned to be careful as well."

I frowned. He was right. I had learned to be like an assassin. It wasn't something I was proud of and not something I ever thought I would have to do. It was one of the ways I was getting money, however, and one of the ways I was able to grow close to Krax.

He changed the subject. "Well, how about you and I go somewhere for a little chat?"

"We could. Or you could go away and leave us alone."

"You know as well I do that isn't going to happen. Be grateful I have a soft spot for you—if I had found one of your friends, they would already be dead."

"Well, they probably would have noticed you coming. They are better about that than I am apparently. I never could sneak up on Ellie, no matter how hard I tried. She is super cautious, but she did grow up with an older brother who liked to pick on her."

"Is it that, or is it because her fiancé betrayed her trust?"

I shot him a look.

Byron chuckled. "Are you still mad about that? It's been three years. You need to move on."

"I will never move on, and you know that."

"Whatever." He jammed the gun into my ribs. "Now move—head up one more floor. You and I have some important business to discuss."

I let out a long deep breath as I moved down the hallway in the direction he gestured with his head. I knew this was not going to end well and prayed that Gabe would get his mother to side with him before it was too late.

Except I had a feeling it was too late and that we needed to get out of there as fast as we could.

# CHAPTER XIX

Ellie

So far there were no signs of Byron or anyone who didn't seem to belong.

Other than us, of course. But the guards didn't notice. We had made our way back up the stairs to see if we could find anyone else out of the ordinary. So far we hadn't seen anything. They were all gossiping or making small talk as drinks were being served in the banquet hall. I also noticed that there was no sign of Cor or Gabe, which meant they either had been kidnapped or they were still talking to his mother. Since the queen wasn't in the banquet hall, I hoped it was the latter.

"This feels like how Zynon was before everything went to shit. I don't like it," Zach commented.

I let out a sigh. "Yeah, it does. I just hope we will catch him before anything happens to all these innocent people."

"I don't know if I would call them innocent, but yeah. I agree."

He had a point there. It didn't seem like anyone was really innocent after you got to know them. But they didn't deserve whatever Byron had in store. No one did. Well, except for Krax maybe.

"Should we check the other floors? I don't think he has set up yet," I said as I scanned the room.

Zach nodded. "Yeah. Knowing him, he will more than likely have a place high up so he can swoop down and save the day. Or cause chaos. Either way."

Just like last time. I let out a sigh as I scanned the room once more. All I could see were Sirians. There were many of them with extraordinary hairstyles and different styles of headdresses. I was surprised, I figured since Gabe seemed to like top hats that there would be more, but apparently not. There were only head wraps, and some had cloth that hid their faces.

Searching a bit more, all I saw was dark hair and grayish skin. It didn't seem that there were any humans here, unless they did their best to disguise themselves. Clearly there weren't any Lyrans as there weren't any cat people, and no one was letting in any Silurians at the moment. I would have assumed Byron would have some humans with him if he were coming down here, but perhaps he didn't need any—perhaps these Sirians would do what he said. It was apparent that the guards were under his thumb. Maybe everyone else was as well.

We headed up the stairs to the next level. There were a few people lingering, mainly servants getting things ready and waiters running down to bring appetizers. I watched as they frantically hurried, trying to make everything perfect even though the queen had requested this banquet last minute. I was impressed by how many people attended and how some of these foods were prepared so quickly. Granted, it had been about twelve hours since we had arrived.

Zach glanced around. "Man, can you imagine growing up here? I can't. This whole palace is larger than a town block in Kaus. And it has far more riches than the entire zone combined."

"I think stuff like this seems more pleasant on the outside than it is on the inside. However, it would have been a bit nicer knowing you were going to have another meal in the day and not have to worry about money. But there is a reason Gabe ran away from it all, however."

"That is true. But goodness, the food smells nice. Can we at least go have a taste?"

I shook my head. "No, they will notice we don't belong if we do that. Once this is over, we can grab some food. I promise."

"You say that, but I have this nagging feeling we aren't going to be getting any dinner."

I rolled my eyes. "Stop worrying about it, or it's going to make you more hungry."

He gave me a sad face, which was strange as he was transformed into a Sirian guard. It had been so long since we had changed like this. The only thing that was similar about him were his eyes and voice, as we couldn't disguise either of those.

"I can't. Food is too good for the soul."

I sighed as we made our way through the hall. So far

there were no signs of Byron or Cor and Gabe. If I remembered correctly, which I did, the queen's room was near the top of the building—which meant we had a lot more stairs to climb. Zach was not going to be happy about that. Especially since he was hungry.

Hadn't these people heard about elevators? I mean, I didn't care for them as they always made me feel trapped and a little queasy. It wasn't as if any place in Kaus had them, and it was rare for many buildings we would go into to have them. The only places that did have them were on the moon and fancy places in some of the capitals. If I heard correctly, the Silurians were the ones who developed them and used them quite frequently in their own zone. Although they seemed to be a very narrow-minded race, they did have some of the most advanced technology that I had ever seen or heard of. Most of it probably was kept secret as well. I was surprised they still rode those weird lizard things called Dracons. Perhaps they simply were better at tracking and could move on different terrain. Or perhaps they liked their weird bark sound.

"How many floors does this palace have?" Zach sighed as we went up another flight of stairs. "I mean, come on…"

"Just think about how many cheeseburgers you can eat to replenish all this energy."

"Oooh, yeah! When we get back to Mu, we're most definitely going to go get cheeseburgers."

"It's a deal. Just no more complaining about stairs. I have a feeling we have quite a few more to climb."

He sighed. "Fine… But there better be milkshakes in my future as well."

I laughed. "And a milkshake. Do you want fries with that?"

"Naturally cheeseburgers come with fries, Ellie. I'm not a monster."

I shook my head. This was a typical Zach conversation. He did love his food, but to be honest, so did I. It was nice being able to eat all we could with Gabe. Before he came along, some days it was hard to find a good meal.

Although it wasn't that long ago, it had seemed like a lot of time had gone by since it was just Zach and I on a mission. Now there were four of us ever since we headed up to Zynon. The moon had been a crazy, quick time. I had almost lost Zach when we were on Zynon, and I couldn't imagine a life without him. I was glad it ended up all right for all of us—glad Krax appeared to distract everyone, otherwise he would have killed Zach to make it look like he had killed Krax. It was a confusing fight, but we were able to make it out of there before anyone had time to stop us.

Except Byron apparently knew exactly where we would run to and already had a plan in place.

Byron was crafty. He knew what he wanted, and he wasn't going to stop at anything to get it. This plan of his had been woven together for years now— generations even. But we had to stop them. We had to destroy his plans before it was too late.

# CHAPTER XX

Zach

That food smelled so good.

Fried fish, octopus balls, jumbo shrimp… I tried to push it all back in my mind, but I was already drooling. I needed the food—I needed to eat. But the farther we went up, the farther away the food would be. A waitress passed me on the stairs. I stared at the contents. A plate full of pot stickers. I thought about grabbing one, but I was able to contain myself.

Because Ellie would scold me for being out of

character.

Was it out of character though? Perhaps the person I was transformed as was as gluttonous as I was. Then they would most definitely be eating a snack like me. Perhaps someone might pass and think, hey why didn't Arnold over there grab a lobster claw? He always grabs a lobster claw. And then people would know I wasn't who I said I was.

That was probably not the case—I just was getting hungry. We had lunch delivered to our room before we all split up again, but that didn't mean I wasn't starving already. It was nearly dinner, and I just knew we were going to have to run for our lives and skip eating. At least by the time we got to Mu, we could grab something to eat.

"Stop thinking about food." Ellie sighed.

"How did you know what I was thinking about?"

"I can see it in your eyes. You make a certain face when you're hungry and are thinking about nothing but food."

"Even while transformed like this?"

She nodded. "Even while transformed like this."

"Fine. I'll think about something else."

I tried but no luck. I really didn't have anything else

to ponder on except our impending doom and failure. Food was a nice way to forget about all that. And it wasn't as if we could play any word games since we were trying not to draw attention.

Stepping up to another level, we checked the hallway for any signs of Cor, Gabe, or Byron. So far there was nothing. The higher we got, the fewer people there were as most were on the first or second floor. We acted as if we were patrolling the palace. No one seemed to notice as we were wearing the outfits and looked the part. No one looked at us in the eye. Most people didn't actually believe that Kausians could transform but thought it was superstition. I had a feeling that down here no one had ever really met a Kausian but only knew what we were because of our eye color. I wished there was a way to make eyes a different color, but there was none.

Then we would be unstoppable.

"So far nothing seems strange, although it's hard to tell since we aren't usually in this palace. Do you think Byron really has something else planned, or do you think he just wants Gabe out of the picture?" I asked.

Ellie shrugged. "I don't know at this point. He really seemed to have it out for him, and I wouldn't put it past him to pause everything he was doing, go out of his way to come here, and take Gabe for himself. Especially since all of us are here together and he knows that. We're his greatest threat."

I let out a long breath. She was right. We knew the truth of what he was plotting, and unless Gabe's mom believed him, we didn't have anyone to take us seriously. There weren't many Kausians left, and those who did survive were hiding as best as they could. There was no way we could find enough of them to get an army going, at least not quickly enough. We were alone in this.

But sometimes it only took one person to stop a war.

"So are we some kind of rogue heroes now? Will they write ballads about us? Have a town named after us with a statue and everything? What would my town be called? Zachsberg?"

She chuckled. "Yeah, I guess that could happen. Maybe. It probably would be a town that only served all you could eat brunch all day every day."

My stomach grumbled. "I finally got my mind to stop thinking about food, and then you bring up brunch? Why would you do that?"

"Sorry, that was my bad. I was just trying to figure out what quirk your little town would have. Mine would have some amazing gun competition and not one that involves killing people."

I nodded slowly. "Yeah, that was not a fun experience at all."

"No, it was not. My competition would be a lot of fun. We would have moving targets and ones where you had to move across an intense terrain. Have to survive on whatever you can find in the wild. Winner gets a day at the spa… I'm starting to like this whole town idea."

"It would be swell."

"Problem is, I doubt anyone would see us as heroes, and we will probably be hunted and murdered for stopping Byron even if we had proof."

"Yeah…"

She really had a point there. No one was going to see us as heroes, or at least I doubted it. I couldn't imagine anyone cheering for us at this point in time. No, most just looked at us with pure hatred. After we killed their favorite person—the person who told them what they wanted to hear. No one liked it when the person who said everything they loved died. No, we would be wanted criminals by then. Not that we weren't already.

We made it up a few more levels. My legs were sore, but I kept pressing on. Mainly because Ellie would yell at me otherwise.

"I think the queen's room is on this level. Keep on the lookout for Gabe and Cor," Ellie whispered as we passed a pair of guards. They didn't say anything but kept on surveilling the area.

I nodded, and we both made our way down the corridors. As we turned down the next hallway, we found Cor with a figure beside him.

Ellie grabbed my arm and pulled me back around the corner. At first I didn't realize why she did it, but then I recognized who that person was.

It was Byron.

He was here, and he had Cor. This was almost the worst-case scenario. The only worse case is if he had already killed Cor, which clearly he hadn't.

"What are we going to do?" I asked in a whisper.

Ellie shook her head. "I don't know—let me think."

"Should we shoot him?"

"It could cause him to shoot Cor right then and there, and that would be a bad thing."

I paused for a second. "Would it though?"

She shot me a look. "That's not funny, Zach."

"Sorry. I'll shut up now."

Ellie pinched the bridge of her nose as she tried to

think. "Gabe wasn't here, so odds are that he's in there talking with his mother in her room. I just don't know what Byron has planned for Cor right now. It could be a similar scenario where Cor disguises himself as someone, or perhaps he's going to wait out there until Gabe comes out and shoots them both."

I glanced around the corner. "It seems Byron is leading Cor somewhere."

"What?" Ellie followed my gaze. "We have to follow them. We can't lose sight of Cor."

"But what about Gabe? All the guards are after him?"

She bit her lip. "You stay with Gabe, and I'll go after Cor. Okay?"

I shook my head. "No, but I think it's the only plan we got."

"Just stay and keep a lookout for Gabe. I'm not sure if he's going to stay at his mother's side all night or what, so we need some eyes on him. I'll follow Cor and try to get him out of this pickle and figure out what Byron's plan is for down here. Sound good?"

There were way too many variables to go wrong in the plan, and I could guarantee at least one, if not all, of them would go wrong. "Again, no. But it's the only plan we got."

"Keep Gabe safe."

"Where are we going to meet up?"

She bit her lip. "Let's meet up either here or at the entrance to the palace. If you aren't here when I come back, that is where I'm assuming you are going to be."

I nodded, hoping I was indeed in one of those two places when she got back. "That works."

"Stay safe."

"You too."

With that, she hurried after Cor and Byron, careful not to be seen by either of them. Once the coast was clear, I stepped into the hallway and paced as if I were patrolling in front of the queen's room. As I moved back and forth for the fifth time, the door to the queen's bedroom opened and smacked my shoulder.

I fell backward and hit the ground. As quickly as I could, I stood up and bowed, keeping my eyes low so she couldn't see them.

"I'm sorry, Your Majesty."

"It is all right. Are you okay?" she asked.

"I'm fine, Your Majesty."

I kept my head down to make sure she didn't see my eyes. After a few moments, she left toward the hallway, and two new guards escorted her. It was apparent Gabe wasn't going with her. He must have still been in the room, hiding from the guards. I watched as the queen was out of view, then opened the door to the bedroom.

# CHAPTER XXI

Gabe

It sounded like there was a kerfuffle outside the door when my mother left, but I stayed in my mother's closet, making sure no guards would come in here and look for me. I heard my mother apologize, so I knew she wasn't in danger. It was probably just some accident.

Hiding in here reminded me when I was a kid as I would always stow away in small places like this, afraid of my uncle and anyone who might want to pick on me that day.

Maybe some things never changed.

This was different than back then, however. I was hiding for the good of the plan and because Byron was trying to kill me. It wouldn't be long now until Cor came in here and we could hide and wait until all this was over together.

At least, that was what I hoped.

A few minutes passed, and there was no sign of Cor. I rocked back and forth, counting the seconds as they went by. Something must have happened, otherwise he would be here by now. It wasn't as if coming in from the other side of the door took that long.

I heard the door creak open, and it felt as if my heart had stopped. Was it him? Or was it a guard looking for me? I didn't hear the person call my name, which Cor would have done. Whoever it was, was trying to be quiet—afraid to get caught.

It was most definitely a guard coming to find me. The question was, how did they know I was here?

I had to come up with a plan. I had a trank gun on me, and I was getting better at using it. I could probably shoot the person and knock them out.

And then what? I didn't know where Cor or the

others were, and it was likely that every guard knew my face and was on the lookout for me. I could try hiding, but then how would I find the others? If they couldn't find me, I would be putting them in danger as well as they would be taking time trying to look for me.

It was a serious dilemma.

I could stay here and hope that no other guard saw this guard come in here. It would be a chance to take, but at least it was some sort of plan. I pulled out my gun and held it in my hands. This was not a familiar feeling. The weapon was cold and smooth, and even though it was only loaded with tranks, it felt deadly in my hands.

The door to the closet opened, and I didn't hesitate to shoot. Whoever it was jumped and moved out of the way.

"Damn it, Gabe, you almost shot me!"

It was Zach.

I got up quickly. "Oh my goodness, Zach! I'm sorry. At least it was only tranks."

"True, but you really need to look before you shoot. Crap, man." He glanced over to where the trank hit the wall. "Also, we need to work on your aim."

That was true. "To be fair, you are still transformed as a guard. If it weren't for your voice, I wouldn't have recognized you."

He glanced down. "That is fair. I would change back into my normal form, but I might not be able to change back to exactly what this guard looks like. I kind of have to be able to see who I'm trying to turn into."

"Whatever you think is best," I commented as I sat down on the couch. "Now, fill me in. What happened to Cor?"

Zach let out a breath. "I'm not entirely sure. When we came up here to search for clues, we found Byron holding Cor at gunpoint. He was leading him down the hall somewhere. Ellie went after him, and I stayed here to keep an eye on you."

I couldn't believe what I was hearing—Byron had Cor. My heart felt as if it were going to leap out of my chest.

"Is he okay? Is he alive?"

"He's alive, but we aren't sure why Byron kept him alive. Ellie is going to try to save him and figure that part out."

At least my love was still alive. But Byron still had him, which was not good. He could torture him or use him as leverage against me. He knew my feelings for Cor, which made me worry even more. What if he tortured Cor to get to me? What if all this was to get to me?

"What in the world is he planning?" I whispered more to me than to Zach.

Zach shook his head. "It beats me. All we found was that the guards were ordered to capture you, nothing else. I assume the moment you stepped on Sirian soil or sand or whatever, he was alerted. But as to what his plan is with the Sirians, I'm not sure. For all we know, he could just be after us."

I shook my head. "No, if that were the case, he would have shot Cor right on the spot. He is going to do something—I just know it."

"What about your mother? Were you able to convince her?"

I nodded. "I did. And she wants all the nations to live in harmony. Although she was rude to you guys when you first met, I think she felt bad."

"We get it. It's a societal thing."

"But she's going to call on all the people tonight to stand by her. She's going to tell them what happened on Zynon and that they needed to stop Byron. As long as her people agree, which we hope will be most of them, we'll have the Sirian army. I doubt even Byron can undo their loyalty to her."

He nodded. "That's good to hear." He bit his lip. "But the fact that Byron is already here is troublesome."

He had a point there. I glanced down at my hands and began to pick at my nails. It was a habit I had gotten from my mother. "You don't think he would hurt her, do you? His brother's own wife?"

Zach shrugged. "I think he's capable of many horrible things, and while I would like to make you feel better, I really wouldn't put it past him."

I frowned. That's what I figured. "We need to keep my mother safe. She's the only thing keeping the Sirians from completely shutting its borders off from the rest of the world."

Zach nodded. "That makes sense to me. When we were patrolling, however, we didn't see anyone who wasn't Sirian. Do you think any of your people are capable of such treacherous acts against the queen?"

I shook my head. "No, I really don't think they are. If Byron was going to kill her, it would be with his own hand."

"Would he though? I mean, he wants their trust. Perhaps he does have someone—perhaps he did convince some Sirians to rebel since she married a human."

"While that is indeed possible, I still think it's quite unlikely. The people were never mad at her for marrying my father but more mad at me for being half human."

"That makes absolutely no sense, but I definitely understand. It's not as if we got to pick our blood, is it?"

I kept forgetting that Zach was half-human since his eyes were still gold. The moment I saw him, I knew he was unique like I was. That was why I picked him out that night. Then he tried to kill me, but luckily now we were good friends. Or at least I liked to think we were.

"Right. We didn't."

Zach clapped his hands together. "Now, what should we do about this pickle we're in? Should we stay here and keep you safe? Or should we go down and make sure your mother is safe, but it would risk us getting caught? Then there is the problem of Cor and Ellie as we have no idea where they could be. Ellie told me to either stay here or meet her at the front entrance if all went to shit."

"Well, I mean, all is probably going to shit, so we could go make sure my mother is safe and then go to the front entrance and get out of there before we're killed. We just need to make sure she tells them everything and they understand how much of a risk Byron is. Then his plan will have failed and there is no use for us to be here."

Zach paced back and forth as if pondering on this dilemma. It was fun to see his mind work even if he was disguised as another person. "You have a good point. That might work. But the question is, will we be able to get close enough to your mother without the guards noticing you are there?"

I glanced over to Mother's wardrobe. "I have just the idea."

# CHAPTER XXII

Cor

Just one plan. That's all I asked for. Just one plan that didn't go completely bonkers. Was that possible? Clearly it wasn't.

Except for Byron. His plans always seemed to go swell.

My jaw was clenched as he led me up two floors. Where in tarnation was he taking me? Was he going to torture me? Could it be any worse than what he had already done to me? He took away everything I loved that day when he forced me to tell Krax the codes to close the shield over Kaus. I had thought he also had been tricked by Krax, only to find out he had been the mastermind behind it all.

I was such a fool.

But I would not be that fool again. No, I would make this right. I had to. There was nothing he could do or say that would make me help him with any other mission he had.

We stopped in front of a door, and he shoved me inside. There were four guards there with a man tied to a chair. As I examined the man some more, I realized what he was.

He was a Kausian.

He wasn't anyone I personally knew growing up or anything, as he more than likely lived in another town. I only came to that conclusion because he was still alive and hadn't been destroyed with everyone else.

The man was wearing tattered clothes, old work boots, and was a bit scruffy in his face. He appeared as if he worked in the fields or possibly at some factory. I had looked into getting some work, but I didn't feel it was worth the pay. I decided if I were going to sell my body for work, I might as well have some fun with it, so

I turned to the saloons instead.

Although the man's eyes were golden, they were also bloodshot as if he hadn't slept in a long while. It was apparent that Byron had kept him prisoner for quite some time now. I wondered if he had a family at home or if he was alone and found himself in this mess. Did Byron kidnap him, or did he lie like he had to me?

"Sit," Byron ordered as he gestured to an unoccupied chair. I took a seat, and some of the guards tied me to the chair. They searched my pockets and took my knives. Ellie was going to be mad as one of them was hers.

I let out a breath as I glared at Byron. "What now? What's your scheme this time?"

Byron laughed as he took a seat across from me. "As if I would tell you. I only brought you here because I needed you out of my way. I do want to know where your friends are though. I presume they are all hiding?"

So he didn't have Ellie or Zach. That was good. "Something like that."

"Well, they will come out eventually, and I can finally get rid of those pesky rats."

"Why do you want to kill them, and yet you are keeping me alive?"

Byron shrugged. "I'm not quite sure. Perhaps it's because I have a soft spot for you, Cor. I did spend all that time teaching you. You were such a curious boy and ambitious. I saw a lot of me in you at the time."

I glared at him. He laughed.

"Or perhaps it was because you helped me destroy your own kind. Or perhaps I just wanted you here to torment this other Kausian I have with me."

I didn't glance over to the other Kausian. I didn't want to see the look on his face—the look of betrayal and anger and rage all wrapped up into one. It was the feeling I had for myself as well.

I was mortified that I had been tricked. I should have known better—I should have just let him kill me. I wanted to go back to the day and make the right decision. But I couldn't, and I had to live with the fact that I picked my own safety rather than my people's.

I could feel tears in my eyes—tears to add to the thousands I had shed for my stupidity. They wouldn't do me any good now, however, and I knew that. So I tried to push them back.

"Aw, are you going to cry because now this Kausian knows the truth about you?" Byron grinned. "Or are you crying because you know you aren't going to be able to get out of this one anytime soon?"

"Perhaps I'm crying because I have to look at your ugly mug."

Byron's hand smacked my cheek. It felt as if something had scratched my face. I had never noticed Byron wore a lot of rings until that moment. I glanced at his hand to find some heavy-duty emerald and diamond rings. I spat out the blood as I had bitten the inside of my cheek.

"You know what would be fun, Cor? How about I let this Kausian take out his anger on you? Don't you think that would be fun?"

I didn't answer but stared down at the ground. I knew I deserved whatever this man would do to me. I wasn't sure Byron would actually do it though, as that would mean his prisoner could try to break free.

"What about Elvira and Zachariah? Did they forgive you? Were you able to make that cute puppy dog face you could always make and get them on your side? Do they realize that you could have sacrificed yourself and their entire home wouldn't have been destroyed?"

I shook my head. "They understand that you were the real culprit behind it all. If it wasn't me, you would just find someone else who knew the codes and coax them into telling them to you. And by coax, I meant threaten and torture.”

“Except there weren’t any other Kausians that knew those codes. Only your parents and you. You were supposed to take over that job, but instead you took my offer in teaching you manners so that you could go to a human university. You had every reason not to trust me, but you let your needs outweigh that. And now here we are.”

I glared at him. “You won’t win, Byron. You won’t be able to destroy all the other races. They will rise up and take you down before your plan works.”

“I don’t need all the different races destroyed. I just need them out of my hair and off the continent so that the humans can take over. I already have had the Silurians retreat, and the Lyrans are in talks with the humans on setting up an attack. But the Sirians, they are a special breed and don’t need to be on Mu. No, if they all moved back here, they would be out of my way.”

I frowned. I didn’t like where this was going. “And how are you going to get them to do that?”

“Don’t you worry your pretty little head about that. You’ll find out in due time. Now, shall we see how angry this Kausian truly is at you? Because I don’t know if you've noticed, but he's been glaring at you something fierce since the moment I mentioned your name."

I didn't look over at him. I didn't want to look at him.

"Do whatever you want. You won't be able to stop the others."

Byron laughed. "Oh, but I will. And I'll start with that pretty little brunette. I'll let you watch as I kill her. Don't you worry. And then Gabe will be soon after that, although I don't think I'll be the one who will take his life."

I narrowed my eyes. "What do you mean by that?"

"You shall see. As for this Kausian…" Byron went over and untied him. "I think he wants to take a few moments to take out his frustrations on you."

I took a deep breath, readying myself for the pain, if that were even possible. The first punch the man made was straight for my nose. Another was in my ribs. He kept hitting me more and more, kicking me in the legs. I spat up blood.

"My sister! My brother! All of them are gone because of you!" the man cried out. "They were going to move in with me until all of it was destroyed. Your own kind is gone because of you!"

As if I didn't know all that already. All my family was gone as well. I knew I deserved the pain—knew I deserved to die—but I had to stop Byron. It was the only thing that was keeping me going.

The man kicked and punched and kicked some more. I expected he wouldn't finish until I was no longer breathing. I suspected Byron would pull him off me before that.

This wasn't the worse beating I had ever had, but it was up there. And I couldn't do anything—not tied to this chair. I wasn't sure if I would even stop him if I could. But I definitely would have used my arms to block the blows to my face.

"That's enough," Byron said. The guards dragged the man off me. "I don't want him to get too many cut marks on his fists to draw suspicion."

Whatever was said after that sounded like it was far away as my ears rang and my vision became blurrier and blurrier. I kept blinking—kept trying to fend off the feeling of passing out. As I felt darkness take hold of me, I saw a familiar face in the background.

"Gabe?"

With that, everything went dark.

# CHAPTER XXIII

Ellie

What should I do? What should I do?

Cor was in there. He was probably being tortured. He could be dead. And I was just standing there in the hallway, not sure what to do next.

Going in without a plan was suicide. Although he was keeping Cor for some weird reason, more than likely because they had history, I had a feeling if I went in there, he would kill me on the spot. No, I had to figure this out.

Which meant I would have to wait until he left.

It was the only logical plan. I couldn't exactly take them all out by myself, as there could be dozens of guards, and I didn't know if Zach was still only a couple of floors below or if he was making his way to the front gate. I took in a deep breath and let it out slowly. I couldn't leave Cor behind. I just couldn't.

But would Cor have done the same for me? Or would he have run? He made sure we were not in Kaus the day of the attack, but he didn't quite stick around to make sure we were all right. I pushed those thoughts to the back of my mind. I couldn't think about such things right then. I had to do what was right.

I stayed in the Sirian form I had, hoping if anyone came out, they would think I was a guard. I didn't know if that was going to work on Byron, however, as he knew what to look for. He was on higher alert than anyone else here.

And he would figure one of us would come looking for Cor.

I couldn't panic. I glanced around to see if there was anywhere I could hide but still keep a good eye on the door. As I searched, I realized what I needed to do. I had to go through the air ducts again. Then I could wait until he left or perhaps see how many people were in there. If it was only him, perhaps I could take him out once and for all. Either way, it was the only chance I had.

I moved around a corner and began to unscrew the vent with the blade of my knife. I prayed that the vent would stay put once I was inside without the screw for at least a little while. I climbed inside and pulled the vent close, transforming back into myself since it no longer mattered. Whether I was a Sirian or myself, it would look pretty suspicious if I came out of a vent.

I could do this. I had to do this.

Crawling toward where the room was, I found myself staring through the vent at Byron and Cor. There were at least half a dozen guards, and they all were armed. There was no way I could jump out of there and shoot them all before one of them pulled out his own gun. I would have to wait until some, if not most, of them left.

There was another person in the room tied up, but it wasn't Gabe. I had no idea who the person was as they did not look familiar. Why would Byron bring another prisoner? I stayed as still and quiet as I could, praying that there wasn't enough light shining into the vent to reveal I was there. Luckily for me, all of Byron's attention seemed to be on Cor. It wasn't lucky for Cor, however. At least he seemed to be in one piece, for the time being.

"Oh, but I will. And I'll start with that pretty little brunette. I'll let you watch as I kill her, don't you worry. And then Gabe will be soon after that, although I don't think I'll be the one who will take his life."

The typical bad-guy-threatening technique. As if we didn't already know that he wanted to kill us all. He really needed to come up with something original. I kept watching, hoping that after that declaration, he would go search for me somewhere, as he didn't realize I was right there within eyesight.

Cor responded. "What do you mean by that?"

"You shall see. As for this Kausian…" Byron went over and untied the other person in the room. "I think he wants to take a few moments to take out his frustrations on you."

That man was a Kausian? Why in the world would he bring a Kausian here? It didn't make sense. Was it to torture Cor? No, there had to be something else. That would be too much hassle just to give Cor a hard time. Byron was going to use the Kausian, but for what? He already had the Sirian guards on his side—he didn't need someone who could shape-shift to persuade them. What exactly was he going to do?

The Kausian went straight for Cor. Byron must have revealed who he was and what Byron claimed he had done. I knew if others found out the truth about Cor, they would go after him as well. I wondered how many over the years had tried to kill him or if they didn't know his involvement. I probably didn't want to know the answer to that.

"My sister! My brother! All of them are gone because of you!" the man cried out. "They were going to move in with me until all of it was destroyed. Your own kind is gone because of you!"

My heart felt as if had dropped into my stomach. I understood what this man felt. My family was also dead, but I didn't blame Cor anymore. It was Byron—this man's frustrations should have been directed at Byron. Perhaps he knew there was no use—Byron would just tie him up again or kill him. Cor, however, was an easy target. And it had been Cor who gave Byron the codes.

If I were honest with myself, I still blamed Cor a little bit. But I knew I would have done the same in his shoes. He wouldn't have given those codes willingly—

no, he had been threatened and tortured. He didn't know they were going to wipe out everyone. I wouldn't have thought anyone would have done anything so cruel either.

But they did. And it was all gone.

The man really went at it on Cor. I held my hand to my mouth to stop from screaming out for him. Cor didn't try to stop him but took every hit as the man screamed at him. His face was quickly bloodied and bruised. The man kept kicking his legs, and I was waiting to hear a crack, but luckily that sound never happened. The man punched Cor in the stomach a few times. Was Byron going to stop him? The man was going to kill Cor if he kept going. I started to reach for my gun.

"That's enough," Byron said. The guards dragged the man off Cor. "I don't want him to get too many cut marks on his fists to draw suspicion."

Cor's head dropped, and he kept on blinking as if he were losing consciousness. He couldn't pass out on me now—I had to get us out of there. I didn't know if I could carry him the entire way.

As my attention was on Cor, I barely noticed what happened next. If it weren't for the words Byron said, I wouldn't have taken notice.

"Now, transform into this man and we shall get this show going," Byron said as he held up a photo to the Kausian.

The Kausian glared at Cor some more and then shifted. If it weren't for the fact my hand was still on my mouth, I would have made a much more audible gasp.

The Kausian had turned into Gabe. That was what he was there for—he was going to do something and pin it on Gabe. But what? Whatever it was, it wasn't going to be good, and we needed to get out of there.

Byron led the Kausian out of the room while the three guards stayed behind with Cor. Cor's head was hanging down, as he clearly had passed out. I prayed I could wake him up and wouldn't have to carry him.

I counted to a hundred to make sure Byron didn't forget something and come back, not to mention he would be well out of hearing range of this room. I readied my gun and turned to kick the screen open.

"Shit, not again!" One of the guards yelled as I shot him. Apparently he was one of the guards that we knocked out when we rescued Gabe. Poor guy, although it did make me smile a bit. The other two tried to reach for their guns, but my friends growing up didn't call me quick-draw Ellie for nothing. I turned and shot them both before they could even aim. They both hit the ground, and I hurried over to Cor.

"Cor, wake up." I slapped his cheeks a little, trying not to hit where there was blood. He didn't respond. I checked his pulse. He was alive all right, just knocked out.

"Well, shit. I guess we're doing this the hard way."

# CHAPTER XXIV

Zach

This was going to be such a long shot that it wasn't even funny.

We had put Gabe in one of the robes that he claimed was for people who had a recent death. It was all white, and there was some kind of hat that had a sheer fabric over the face to hide the tears one would shed while mourning. Apparently Sirians wore white when they mourned for someone, opposite to the black that humans wore. Kausians didn't have a color they wore, as we didn't even have that much choice when it came to clothing.

He was technically wearing women's clothing, as it was the robe his mother wore when his grandmother died. No one would notice he was a man, however, as he was rather thin and because his face was masked.

"My mother should recognize this outfit and know it's me. As for the others, well, many don't want to make eye contact with someone grieving as they think it's bad luck, so they'll ignore me."

That made little sense, but at least we had a plan now. Now hopefully no one downstairs would notice my eyes and we would be set.

"Are we sure this is going to work?" I asked as we made our way to the hallway. There was no one outside the chambers, as I assumed Cor dealt with them before getting captured by Byron.

He shrugged. "I have no idea, but I think it's the best plan we can come up with on such short notice."

Gabe had a point. I really wished Ellie were here. She was better at plans than I was. She was quick to think of every possible thing to go wrong. I called it anxiety, but she called it survival instincts. Either way, her bright mind got us out of a lot of scrapes.

I followed Gabe out into the hallway, glancing around for any signs for Cor and Ellie. It seemed Ellie hadn't quite saved Cor yet. It was too bad, as this might have gone more smoothly if we were all together. I didn't like being separated—you never knew what was going on with the other people and were constantly worried, which made it hard to focus on one's own mission. Nevertheless, sometimes we had to split up.

We made our way down the stairs, which I hated. Ellie had better succeed in her mission as I did not want to climb back up these bad boys again tonight. Hopefully we would finish what we needed, and then we could be on our merry way and gone from anywhere Byron could get us. I had a feeling, however, these stairs weren't through with me quite yet.

Because everything was going to explode in our faces.

Everything already had gone to shit, that was clear enough. Byron had Cor, Ellie was going to try to save him, everyone was after Gabe, and I was transformed into a Sirian, which was illegal and could get me killed. Granted, most people wanted to kill us anyway, so it didn't matter. But something about being killed for using our birth powers seemed wrong. I would rather be killed for something heroic—at least, that was my opinion.

"So repeat the plan to me," I leaned over and whispered to Gabe as we made it down about five flights.

"We're going to go downstairs, I'm going to pull my mother aside and tell her that Byron is here and he is going to do something, and she will tell everyone what is going on right away instead of waiting a bit for people to settle down and such. Usually there is a sequence of events before leading up to a speech, which she was going to follow. Now this way we can try to get people to understand what is going on before he tries anything."

I nodded. That all made sense. "In theory, right?"

He let out a sigh. "In theory, yes. It just all depends on what Byron has in store for us."

I hated Byron with a growing passion. Each moment that passed, the more the anger grew. How was he able to do everything that he had done so far? Why was he so powerful that he could manipulate people and get them to do what he wanted? Was it truly just fear? Or did they agree with his beliefs? I supposed it depended on the zone. The Silurians wanted power, and he gave them that until he betrayed them. Sirians seemed to want to keep to themselves, so how was he going to betray them? How was he going to make their world come crashing down?

"At least your mother listened to you. That's a good start. Even if it takes some time, she will hopefully convince the people of what kind of man Byron is."

Gabe bit his lip. "I hope so. Many people are still set in their ways, but I have hope. Even after all of this is over, there is still a lot of work to do in all the nations. My sister will have to take charge, and I hope she is as skillful at doing so as my mother."

I glanced over at him. "What? You don't think you'll stick around to help rule?"

He shook his head. "No, or at least I doubt it. I think they'll all do a better job at it without me around. Maybe eventually I can come back, but probably not. Many of the people still hate me, and I have learned to live with that. What matters is who I am on the inside and how I view myself."

A feeling I too had to come to terms with when I was younger. "Well, I like you, Gabe. I'm glad we're friends."

Gabe smiled. "Thank you. And likewise, Zach. I

think you are very sweet and kind. There aren't many people out there who are as empathetic."

That made me grin a little as we stepped up to where the banquet was being held. It seemed that more people had arrived as the place was jam-packed with people. Although there were many Sirians, all with fantastic robes and dresses and hairstyles I didn't even think was possible, there was still a lot of room to maneuver. There were performers dancing in various spots of the room as I heard a string instrument play from somewhere I couldn't pinpoint. Some of the dancers had fans, and others had swords, and some had nothing at all.

In the center of the banquet hall was a large marble fish that stood almost two stories tall, as the ceilings had gone up at least three stories. Large chandeliers hung in the air, glowing from some sort of light source that wasn't light bulbs like it would be on Mu. I had no idea what the light was coming from, but it shone like the moon.

Gabe smacked my side, and I realized I had my mouth open. I quickly closed it and smiled to him. I couldn't tell what kind of face he was making under the fabric, but I had a feeling he was laughing at me.

As we ventured through the large room, searching for his mother, I caught a whiff of some of the food that was being served. There were waiters and waitresses with plates of food. People were grabbing crab puffs, octopus balls, and deep fried shrimp. My stomach rumbled, and I quickly snatched one of the shrimp.

I turned to Gabe. "Don't tell Ellie, but I'm starving."

"Mum is the word. You need your energy, especially if we will have to make a run for it."

I nodded. He understood. Food was important, especially when you were constantly on high alert and your adrenaline was off the charts. I took a bite of the shrimp. My eyes closed in ecstasy. It was crunchy on the outside with a soft texture on the inside. The normal bland shrimp flavor brought out the herbal mix that was in the batter of the crust. There were plenty of different flavors, all unique, and yet they came together in perfect harmony.

This was the best shrimp I had ever had.

My theory that all the good seafood was kept in the Sirian Zone was correct. All the worst quality was sent to the other zones. That was why I didn't like it as much as I did here. I definitely wanted more, but I would wait. While it was hard to run on an empty stomach, sometimes it was even harder on a full one.

We wandered some more, searching for the queen. Eventually we found her talking to two gentleman with graying hair, which contrasted with their normal dark black hair. The moment the queen saw Gabe, she stopped talking to the men. Her eyes went wide when she realized he was wearing her clothing.

She turned to the men. "Will you excuse me just one moment? I have an urgent matter to discuss with this person."

# CHAPTER XXV

Gabe

My mother took me aside and hissed. "Gabriel, what do you think you are doing? You look ridiculous in that outfit."

"I didn't want anyone to recognize me, and I figured since it was your dress, you would still be able to spot me."

"Well, I suppose you are correct. But what are you doing down here? I thought you were going to stay upstairs?"

"Mother, Byron is here. He's going to do something probably soon. We need to get the truth out to these people before it's too late. Can you make your speech now instead of later?"

She frowned a little. "You know how these people like to play by the rules, Gabe. If I interrupt them now, they might find it rude and ignore my request."

"I understand that, but there's a lot at stake right now. Byron could come any second and attack. We need to have people understand what he's capable of."

Mother let out a sigh but then finally nodded. "Fine. I can do it. I think it would be more effective if we wait, but if what you say is true, we may not have much time."

I smiled. "Thank you."

"But afterward, promise me you'll go up to my room and wait there along with your friends. I don't want any of you getting hurt. We need to sit down and really discuss what has happened. And if I find Byron, I'll be having quite the word with him as well, and I'll be throwing him in prison until we can get this all sorted."

"Of course, Mother."

She turned and began to head where the grand stairs were—the place anyone stood if they were to give a speech so everyone could see and hear them. The sound in that spot echoed through the entire room, and even in the far back one could hear whoever was speaking.

I ventured over to Gabe, who was now eating some octopus balls. He placed the last one in his mouth and wiped his hands on the scaled armor of the guard uniform he was wearing.

"So? What did she say?"

"She's going to make a speech right now. Afterward, we have to go up to her room and wait. I just hope that we're able to find Ellie and Cor before then."

Zach made a sigh. "I don't want to go up those stairs."

I chuckled. "Well, I promise once we're up there, we can order room service."

"Oooh, it's a deal."

My mother made her way across the room, getting stopped every couple of yards or so by someone wanting to discuss something. She did her best to get out of the conversations, but it was still taking a while for her to get up to the platform.

I glanced around for Byron. There still was no sign of him, which I didn't know whether that was good or bad. If he was here, then I might know what he was up to, but then he could easily stir the crowd to believe him.

Perhaps that was what he was going to do. He was going to stand in front of everyone and try to make them think my mother was lying. That I was lying. And then turn them against us.

I prayed silently to the goddess that my mother would get up there before it was too late.

I felt someone tug on my robe. I glanced down to find Kishiko. She stared up at me.

"Brother, why are you wearing that outfit? Did someone die?"

I held a finger to my lips. "Shh, don't let anyone hear you."

"Why not?" she asked, folding her arms.

"Because I'm not supposed to be here."

She looked at me confused. "It's your party. Why shouldn't you be here?"

I saw Zach laughing out of the corner of my eye. I shook my head. "I… It's grown-up things. But I'm going to surprise everyone later that I'm here, okay? Like a surprise party. You don't want to ruin the surprise for everyone, do you?"

She shook her head. "No, I don't. I'll keep your secret, brother."

"Thank you."

As I was distracted by my sister, my mother had made her way to the top of the stairs. She took her glass and used a spoon to make a loud tinging noise to gather everyone's attention.

"Hello, everyone! Please, if I can have your attention."

The room went silent, and the koto music stopped. All the dancers also stopped moving as my mother waited for everyone's attention.

Kishiko tugged on my robe again. "I want to see Mother. Can you pick me up?"

I smiled and nodded as I picked her up so she could see over everyone's heads. I noticed Zach smile as he watched us.

"As you all know, my son Gabriel is back in the Sirian Zone. While I know a lot of you dislike him and disagreed with his birth, I have some important news that was given to me by him. It has to do with the attack on Zynon."

There was a murmur through the crowd. It was clear that all of them already knew of the news that had been reported. None of them would believe that it was fake —they would all take Byron's word for it. I took a deep breath, waiting for my mother to continue.

"In the official report, we were told that the leader of the Silurians, Krax, gave an order to shoot everyone at the poker tournament. Byron was then said to have killed Krax and helped stop the Silurians from killing any more people. That was what witnesses also reported, but there was something else going on that night—something that only a few people know."

As my mother started to explain, a figure stepped down the stairs behind her. Those stairs only led to the throne room—a place no one was allowed to go to unless she was in there.

Which meant a guard let them in.

As the figure grew closer, I stared at them, confused. It couldn't be possible—the person behind her couldn't be who they appeared like.

Because that person looked like me.

My mother turned to the person. "Gabriel? What are you doing here? How did you—"

She didn't finish what she was going to say. The person who appeared like me raised their gun and fired a bullet straight into her heart. The sound of the gunshot echoed through the chamber. In that moment, I watched as the person that I cared about most collapsed to the ground, red blood pooling around her body. There was silence for a moment before everything turned into chaos.

# CHAPTER XXVI

Ellie

An unconscious body was so very heavy.

It took me a bit to figure out the best way to carry Cor. I ended up discarding the top layer of the guard uniform, as they were hard to maneuver in, given I was smaller than the guard I had transformed into. With the armor gone, I was now in some simple pants, shirt, and some boots that were a bit on the large size. I checked the other guard's feet, and one of them had a smaller shoe size that was closer to my own. I took his shoes, as going barefoot was sometimes not a good idea.

I flung Cor over my shoulder, his arm pinned across my chest and my arm around his leg, grabbing his wrist so that he would stay as secure as possible. I did my best not to drop him, but with every step I took in the corridors, the more he felt as if he were going to slip out of my arms. This was not a good situation, as if some guards saw us and pursued, there was no way I would be able to get us to safety.

Cor definitely was muscular, which added a lot of weight. I apparently needed to get a bit stronger and would definitely work on my arm strength in the near future. With all the stairs we had climbed, I knew my leg strength was improving.

Speaking of stairs. I needed to somehow get this big oaf down to where Zach and Gabe were hopefully waiting for us. At least with all three of us, we could move Cor a lot easier. Hopefully he would wake up soon so we didn't have to, but I wasn't sure how long that was going to take.

I let out a sigh as I came to the stairwell. At least I didn't have to climb up the stairs, but going down wasn't going to be much easier. I had to make sure I didn't drop him, for starters, as that would not end well.

I would have hated to have made it this far and then bash his skull in on the stairs with my own two hands.

I nudged Cor with my shoulder. "Come on, wake up, Cor."

He didn't move. That Kausian really did a number on him. He definitely hadn't held back as he delivered blow after blow. I understood how he felt, as I had punched Cor the moment I laid eyes on him. But then I broke down in the middle of a crowded walkway. Looking back on it, I was a bit embarrassed. But all the emotions from the past three years came flooding back to me. It was unbearable.

I still couldn't believe that Byron had brought a Kausian down here and had him transform into Gabe. To what purpose could that have been for? How did he get the Kausian to do as he wished? I had a feeling it was through some threatening manner. Maybe he had a loved one that Byron had locked away somewhere. It was highly ironic that he took so much of his anger out on Cor when he was being used by Byron in the exact same way. But perhaps he knew he couldn't attack Byron and took out his frustrations on Cor.

Either way, I prayed that Gabe and Zach were still only a couple of levels below us so I could get some help. Zach was large and muscular and could easily carry Cor compared to me. Even if Cor woke up, he might be in a lot of pain to walk, as the man kicked him a few times in the leg. I had felt around before carrying him, but nothing seemed broken. It just appeared a bit bruised and swollen, which would slow him down. But at least he could put some weight on it and I didn't have to carry him on my back once he woke up.

Slowly but surely, we made it down to the next level. There were no guards on the stairs, thank goodness. I was afraid, though, that there were still guards patrolling the level Zach and Gabe were hopefully on, as it was where the queen's room was. Potentially they had escorted the queen down the stairs, but I knew I was never that lucky.

So, more than likely, there were a few on that level, making sure some troublemakers weren't breaking into the queen's suite.

I sighed as we made it down a couple more steps. My back was aching, and I could feel my muscles starting to tire. I didn't want to stop, however, as it was hard enough trying to situate Cor on my back. No, I had to keep pressing forward, no matter how much my body hurt.

Cor owed me big time.

I made it to the next level and peered down the corridor. There wasn't any sign of people, thank goodness. I took a deep breath and prepared my body for the next flight of stairs.

"I swear to the goddess, Zach, if you aren't on the next level, I'm going to slap you."

There was no way I was going to be able to take Cor all the way down to the main level. If I had to, I would try to find the strength, but it would leave me vulnerable and tired if we needed to run. I doubted Cor could run at this point. We were in a worse pickle than I could have ever imagined.

I just prayed that the situation didn't get worse.

I knew it would. It always would.

The next level more than likely had guards. As I made it to the last couple of steps, I pulled out my gun with my left hand, which was my free hand. I hunched over to make sure Cor was still sturdy. Although it would have been nice to use both arms to keep him on my back, I needed to be ready for anything.

Stepping down to the last few steps, I peered around the corner. Sure enough, I found two guards with their backs turned to me. I pinned my wrist into my side and aimed at the closest one. Thank goodness there wasn't much of a kick for tranks. The man fell over, passed out. The other guard turned, and before he could pull out his gun, I shifted and shot him as well. He fell to the ground next to his patrol buddy.

I kept my gun out in case there were more guards. After waiting a couple of moments, there was no sign of anyone else. I proceeded to carry Cor to the room that Zach and Gabe were supposed to meet us at.

I opened the door to the queen's room.

It was silent. There was no sign of Zach or Gabe.

"You guys? Are you in here hiding?"

There was no sound. I cursed under my breath. "You have got to be fucking kidding me."

I closed the door and set Cor on the couch closest to the entrance. He didn't wake up.

"Where did you go, Zach? Why did you leave this room?"

I let out a sigh as I sat down to catch my breath. What was I going to do? It was going to take all my strength to go all the way down the stairs with Cor on my back. I could wait here for their return, but what if something happened that required for us to escape? Then I would have to get down the stairs even faster. What needed to happen was for Cor to wake up, but that wasn't exactly easy when he had been knocked out cold.

I turned to Cor and slapped him again. There was no response. I glanced around and found a few perfumes. Perhaps strong scent would help him wake up. I grabbed one bottle and opened it under his nose. No response. I tried half a dozen different bottles when finally he began to stir.

Smacking him in the face, I yelled, "Cor, wake up! I need you to wake up!"

He slumped back over and passed out again. I sighed. I couldn't spend any more time here. I quickly poured a few drops of the perfume on my shoulder where his head would be and picked him up and swung him around my back. Hopefully eventually the smell would get him to wake up all the way.

Gathering him up on my back, I headed down the stairs, cursing as much as felt necessary along the way.

# CHAPTER XXVII

Cor

I woke up to the strangest sensation.

First off, all I could smell was jasmine. It smelled like my mother's garden, growing up. She used to pick them and make potpourri. Sometimes she would sell it at the market for some extra money to buy me clothes as a kid. I always loved the scent, and every time I went to a fancy shindig with Gabe, some woman or another was wearing a perfume made of it. It took everything for me not to break down crying.

The second thing that was off was that I felt as if I were swinging a little. It was almost like a hammock but not quite. It wasn't like being flung on the back of a horse either. My eyes flickered open, and I found myself staring down at someone's ass and some stairs. Someone was carrying me, and I had no idea who it was. This, of course, caused me to flinch and jump a little.

"Whoa! Stop!" Ellie yelled. "Otherwise we both go straight down on the stairs, and personally I don't want to do that today."

"I should have recognized your butt."

Ellie let out an exasperated breath. "Shut up or I'll toss you down the stairs."

I couldn't help but laugh. "Just put me down, will you? I need a moment."

"All right, but be careful. That guy did a number on you."

She put me down, and the moment my left leg hit the ground, I grimaced. That was right, the Kausian had tried to beat me to a pulp. I tried to recall everything that occurred. Byron had captured me and got that guy to beat me up, all for shits and giggles. Then something happened, but it was all a blur. I sat on the ground and pulled up my pant leg up to examine the damage.

Ellie knelt beside me. "I don't think it's broken, just a bit bruised."

"That's good." I sighed as I pulled my pant leg down. "What happened? How did you rescue me? Where are the others?"

Ellie took a seat next to me. "Well, first, Byron left you with some guards. He had that Kausian who transformed into Gabe. I'm not sure what he's going to do there, but it can't be good. Then I was in the vents part of the time you were being beaten. After Byron left, I jumped out and used my tranks, of which I'm running low on. I did retrieve your weapons, by the way. I put them back where you typically keep them. Except the knife you stole—I took that one back."

Damn, I was hoping she didn't find out about that. I patted around. Sure enough, they were exactly where I kept them.

"Then I carried you back to where Gabe and Zach were supposed to be, but they weren't there. I told Zach if anything happened, to meet us at the front gate, so I assume that's where they are headed. And that's pretty much everything that has happened since you passed out."

I nodded. Seemed about right—nothing was going according to plan. "How long ago did Byron leave?"

She shrugged. "I don't know? Half an hour. I think we need to get a move on it before he does whatever he's going to do. I do know it involves that Kausian turning into Gabe though."

My eyes widened. "That wasn't a dream? I really did see Gabe?"

"Yeah, well at least that Kausian turning into him. I assume he's going to use Gabe to make people mad or something. I'm not sure. Either way, it can't be good. We need to get down there before it's too late. Or find the others and run as fast as we can. Either way, we have a few flights of stairs ahead of us."

Right. This day was getting better and better. What would Byron need a Kausian to transform into Gabe for? It wasn't as if those people liked him, so he wasn't using him to persuade anyone. No, he had something more sinister.

I turned my attention back to Ellie. "Do you know if Gabe was able to convince his mom?"

Ellie shook her head. "No idea. When I got back down, they were gone, and when I went after you, Gabe was still talking to her alone."

Great. We didn't know if we had her on our side or not.

"Then I guess we should go down there and find out."

I began to stand, but the pain in my leg was too much for my full weight. Ellie quickly stood and helped me up.

"Whoa there. Just put your arm around me and we will get down the stairs together. Although a pain, at least I'm not carrying you. You are heavy, you know that?"

Of course Ellie always had to crack a joke when there was chaos all around. It was probably her coping mechanism, as it was mine sometimes. "How many more flights do we need to get down?"

"At least seven."

"You carried me over halfway down?" I asked, not believing that was possible.

She nodded. "Yup. I'm beyond tired right now, but my drive and not wanting to die is keeping me going."

That was impressive. I didn't know if I could have such determination.

I nodded down the stairs. "Well, let's get at it."

We carefully made our way down the stairs. It wasn't

too hard with my arm around Ellie, and she was quite strong for her size. I had no idea how she was able to carry me as far as she had. I guessed it was true what they said about women and adrenaline.

"Thank you," I whispered.

Ellie turned to me. "Hmmm?"

"For not leaving me. Most people would have after what I have done."

She shook her head. "I'm not leaving you, Cor."

I smiled a little and wondered how much of that was true? Would she really always be there to rescue me? Or did she simply do it because she was there? If she had to make a choice between saving me and saving her own life, would she take it? I didn't feel anyone would risk their life for me. I wasn't worthy of such a sacrifice. I couldn't rely on anyone because I didn't deserve their help—that much I knew.

Byron should have let that Kausian kill me. It would have been the right thing to do. I earned it. I was the reason that man's family was gone. I was the reason my own family was gone. I didn't earn the life I had been given since that day.

I should have died with the rest of them. I knew that. I always knew that.

We kept making our way down the stairwell. My leg was practically screaming at me to stay off it, but I didn't have a choice. As we went down and down, my vision kept getting blurrier from the pain. I kept focusing on the scent of jasmine that came from Ellie and trying to ignore the pain in my leg. It sort of worked.

As we made it to the third floor, we heard a gunshot. Both of us stopped in our tracks. I had a feeling we both expected more shots than that, just like on Zynon, but there weren't any. It was just the one, and then the palace erupted in screams.

"What in the goddess's name was that?" Ellie whispered. "Should we check it out, or should we keep going?"

I shook my head. "I don't know."

# CHAPTER XXVIII

Gabe

It felt like time had stopped, and all I could see was the chaos around me. I couldn't move. There were no sounds. There was only the sight of blood and my mother on the ground.

My ears were ringing, and I wasn't sure why. It was as if someone was yelling in my ear. After a few moments, time started back up again and everything felt as if it were rushing to catch up with the moments that had slowed down.

It was my sister—she was screaming in my ear.

"Mommy! No!"

I didn't know what to do, but I knew I had to get out of there. Luckily, I was hiding under this mourning veil, but I assumed everyone was going to be searched once they ran out these doors. Everyone would be looking for me. I had no way out of there.

And I didn't know what to do with my sister. At the moment, she was a liability. If people saw her—recognized her as the princess—they would notice it was me who held her. And I had a feeling they would think my intention was to hurt her.

That was far from the truth. I would never hurt my sister. Or my mother. But they wouldn't believe that. I couldn't believe them. Not after what I had seen.

A Kausian had transformed into my likeness and killed my mother in front of all these people.

I was going to go after him, but he disappeared and transformed into a different face as he stepped into the crowd.

It couldn't have been Cor. Could it have been? Even if Byron kidnapped him and tortured him, he wouldn't kill my mother, would he have?

No, I had to believe it was some other Kausian. There

were still many out there. Byron probably forced one of them to do it. Just like he did last time.

Zach grabbed my arm. "We have to get out of here before someone recognizes you."

I nodded and turned. My sister was still screaming, and I wanted to tell her to stop crying, but I couldn't. How awful would it be to tell someone to stop crying after they saw their own parent killed right in front of their eyes. I pushed my own sobbing back, knowing it would only cause more problems.

I had to be strong. I had to keep going. I had to fight for my mother's beliefs.

Byron was in for it now. I would not let him get away with this. I would avenge my mother if it were the last thing I did.

I didn't know what to do with my sister as we made our way through the banquet hall. So far, no one really paid her much mind as everyone was screaming and trying to save their own skin, but it was only a matter of time. I didn't know whom to trust, but I had to give her to someone. She wasn't safe with me.

I couldn't trust the guards as they were in with Byron. Whether they knew he was going to do this, I had no idea, but I couldn't exactly believe they were innocent. The rest of the people here were strangers, and I had no idea who was on our side or not.

What should I do? I had to make sure she stayed safe.

I couldn't exactly leave her alone either, as she was just a child and would get stampeded if she were on the ground. I was glad she had found me before the chaos —otherwise I had no idea what would have happened.

Suddenly someone grabbed me and tugged me aside. I was about to pull my gun out on them when I recognized his face.

"Krisian?" I asked.

He nodded. "Yeah. I thought it was you. We need to get you out of here."

I didn't know what to do or say. This man, a boy when I knew him, was the so-called friend who used to come over and act sweet to my mother, only to treat me as if I were trash. He would take his fill of food and wear fancy clothes but not even talk to me the entire time. While he was one of the few who did come over to play with me, so to speak, I wouldn't exactly call it a lasting friendship.

He grabbed my wrist, and I pulled back. "No. I don't trust you."

Krisian stepped forward. "Look, if I were going to do

anything to hurt you, I would have called the guards over here by now. I want you and the princess to be safe, okay? I know it wasn't you who shot the queen. You would never do that, and I was one of the closest people to where she was standing. I saw his eyes."

At what I would consider the worst possible moment to step up to us, Zach came over. "What's going on here?"

Krisian appeared as if he were going to attack Zach. I didn't know if it was because he had gold eyes or if it was because he appeared like a guard, but he pulled his arm back. I reached out with my free hand and stopped him.

"Wait, this is my friend and not the man who killed my mother." I glanced around, hoping no one heard me say mother. "I mean, the queen. It was a different Kausian who did it. I'm not sure who, however."

Krisian eyed Zach for a long moment, then turned back to me. "We have to be quick before someone takes notice of us standing here."

"Oh, and what do you have in mind? I can't exactly run out the front when the guards are more than likely rounding everyone up."

"Well, first we're going to meet up with my wife. I

can see her near the entrance to the banquet hall. She'll take the princess to safety and say she saw her on the ground and had to protect her. Meanwhile, the three of us will head up somewhere to hide."

The plan at least included my sister's safety, so I couldn't exactly argue on that point. But I didn't like the sound of the rest. "Up? We will be trapped. How exactly will I be able to get to safety that way?"

"All the guards will be down here, hoping everyone doesn't escape. They will take some time before they start searching floors. Luckily, they are looking for you in a different color robe, but they won't find you. The last place they'll look is your room as it wouldn't make sense you would go back there. We will hide there and then come up with a plan. Now hurry, we don't have much time before they close off the stairwells."

Krisian stared off toward his wife, and I quickly followed suit. Zach ran beside me.

"Are you sure we can trust this guy?"

I shook my head. "I don't know, but I think it's the best shot we have for getting out of here."

"Fair enough."

We made it to where his wife was waiting for him.

"Yolanda, I'm going to help this person. Please take

the princess and get to safety." Krisian instructed his wife.

She shook her head. "Where are you going? I don't understand."

"It's important. Please just take the princess and run."

"No!" Kishiko screamed. "I want to stay with my brother."

I scanned around. No one had noticed what she said. "Shh, Kishiko. You have to go with her. It isn't safe."

"No! I don't want to be alone!"

I had to use all my will not to cry. "Please go. You'll be safe. I promise I'll come back to you, okay? But first I have to avenge our mother. Can you stay here for me so I may come home one day?"

Her eyes were full of tears. Finally she shook her head yes and let Krisian's wife take her. I kissed her forehead.

"I love you, Kishiko. Until we meet again."

Krisian kissed his wife goodbye, and she hurried toward the front of the palace. Krisian nodded toward the stairwell on the far side.

"We'll go this way. Hurry."

Zach glanced around. "I'm going to search for Cor and Ellie down here. They may have already made it down and are searching for us. If some time passes and I can't find them, I'll make it back up to you."

I shook my head. "I won't leave you alone. What if you get noticed?"

"No one will notice me since I'm in guard's clothing and look like them. They are looking for you anyhow. Now go. Get to safety."

I nodded and turned to Krisian. Together, we headed toward the stairwell.

# CHAPTER XXIX

Zach

I did not see any of this coming.

Byron had found some Kausian and had them transform into Gabe to kill his mother. Why didn't he just kill her some other way? Why had he wanted her dead in general? That was a matter to figure out later. First, I had to find where Cor and Ellie were.

I presumed Byron was somewhere nearby, making sure everything was going according to plan, which meant Ellie had her chance to rescue Cor. That is, if it wasn't Cor who shot the queen. I highly doubted it, unless he was using Ellie as a hostage or something.

My heart skipped a beat. What if that was it? What if Byron had Ellie tied up somewhere and forced Cor to kill the queen?

Cor wouldn't do that, would he? I could definitely see Byron using Cor like that and making him choose between Ellie's life and Gabe's mother. It was devious and disgusting to think about. But it wouldn't be the first time Byron had stooped so low.

And it would be icing on the cake for him to make Cor choose like that.

I doubted Cor would do it though. Not after everything. It had to be someone else—another Kausian. There would have been too many other variables for Byron to risk otherwise.

I kept on searching for them. That couldn't be what had happened. No, they both were fine. It was just some other Kausian he used and threw away. That was Byron's thing. I wondered how many other ones he had used and abused. We would make him pay for using our kind like that and destroying our home in the process.

People were still running around, freaking out that there were guards everywhere trying to find Gabe. No one had noticed my eyes, as they weren't really looking at me, which was good. I didn't want to die like this. Not that any other way would really be that much better in the long run.

I was surprised by how many people didn't notice that the princess was crying. No one went to help her— no one seemed to care about anyone else but themselves. It was sickening to hear the princess cry like she had. She was just a kid, and she had to witness her mother killed. It wasn't right.

Luckily a friend of Gabe's saved us. I didn't know what we were going to do until he showed up. I had a feeling Gabe didn't want to simply set his sister down and walk away, so it was good he was able to find someone to trust. It definitely made me feel better.

I descended the stairs to the main floor lobby. Guards were at the doors, ushering people outside to safety, along with checking everyone's IDs and looking for Gabe and probably us Kausians. We definitely couldn't go out that way, which meant Ellie and Cor were somewhere else.

Scanning the room, I acted as if I were helping people go to the front when really, I was keeping an eye out for Cor and Ellie. For all I knew, they could have transformed into someone else and blended in. Or they were the ones who shot the queen.

No. It wasn't them. I had to keep telling myself that.

But where were they? Did they stay up in the queen's room? Ellie said if she didn't see me and Gabe there, she would come down here. Had something happened? Was she still trying to rescue Cor? Or had they both been injured?

I took a deep breath and tried to stay calm, but the fact that everyone around me was running around freaking out did not help. I felt so crowded and yet so alone at the same time. The world around me was spinning, and I felt as if I were about to have a panic attack.

That was when I heard Ellie's voice.

"Psst, Zach! Over here!"

I turned to find Ellie and Cor hiding behind a pillar that was off to the side near the stairs—the ones opposite to where Gabe had gone up. Ellie was back to her normal form and was keeping Cor steady. Cor did not look good. His face was bruised and blooded, and he wasn't putting any weight on his leg.

I hurried over to them, relief filling my insides.

"What happened?" both Ellie and I asked at the same

time.

I shook my head. "No time to explain—we need to get up to Gabe's room and figure all this out."

Cor and Ellie made a face as Cor commented, "Are you crazy? We need to get out of here."

I motioned to everything going on. "If you can't tell, there is a bit of a situation down there. They are checking everyone who leaves. We can't get out of here."

Ellie pursed her lips. "He has a point. Is Gabe already up there?"

I nodded. "Yeah, some friend took him."

Cor narrowed his eyes. "Friend?"

I shrugged. "If the guy wanted to harm Gabe, then he would have done so already. He had the opportunity to notify the guards where Gabe was. Instead, his wife took the princess and let us escape. Or let Gabe escape while I searched for you two."

Ellie nodded to the stairs. "Then let's get going before someone sees us and they block the stairs."

Cor cursed under his breath. "Back up the fucking stairs."

I hurried to the other side of Cor. "What happened here?"

Ellie eyed the people that still made up the area. "Let's get somewhere more secluded, then we can exchange stories."

I nodded as we helped Cor hobble toward the stairwell. I stopped and bent down a little. "I think this will go better if you just hop on my back. I'm pretty strong—more so than Ellie."

"Hey, I'll have you know I carried him unconscious down a few flights of stairs."

"I know you are strong, Ellie, but you probably didn't move as fast as I could have."

She shrugged. "Fair enough. Your turn to carry him."

Cor got onto my back, and we began to ascend the stairwell. There was no one going up or coming down. Apparently, everyone who was left already tried to vacate the palace.

Which meant guards would start searching for us soon.

"All right," I said. "Do you want to start or shall I?"

"I followed Byron and Cor," Ellie began. "And Byron had another Kausian with him. He let the Kausian beat Cor into a pulp, as you can see, and then the Kausian turned into Gabe. I have a feeling whatever that was for is what the chaos was about."

"Ah. So it was another Kausian. I didn't think it could have been either of you, but I had my worries." I took in a deep breath and sighed. "Before the queen could tell everyone the truth about what happened, the Kausian, appearing as Gabe, killed the queen in front of everyone, causing them to believe Gabe killed his own mother."

There was silence for a moment as Cor and Ellie processed this information. Cor laughed a defeated laugh.

"So we're screwed is what you're saying. The entire world is against us, and we have no one backing us up as we go after Byron."

I nodded slowly. "That pretty much sums it up, yeah. The Sirians will be looking for Gabe, Byron for all of us, the Silurians for some reason for Ellie and I, and, well, I don't know what the Lyrans think of us, but we will probably soon find out."

"They have no real reason to hate us; however, I don't know how we would be able to talk to anyone important. Even if we went to their zone or leader, they would think we were lying. But I bet Byron already has them wrapped around his finger for one reason or another. He seems to have everyone wrapped around his finger," Cor mumbled.

Ellie commented, "We will have to figure out what to do about Byron later. First, we need find how to get out of this zone. The guards will be at all the exits, and once everyone is gone, they are going to start searching all the rooms and do a huge sweep. We won't be able to stay hidden for long."

I just prayed that wouldn't happen too quickly and we could get our thoughts on straight. But I had a feeling that was not going to happen anytime soon.

# CHAPTER XXX

Gabe

My greatest fault was probably the fact I was too trusting. I knew that, and yet in the past week or so, I trusted a bunch of people who almost killed Cor or me. I had trusted Zach, and he almost killed me, I had trusted both Zach and Ellie, and they were about to kill Cor. I trusted I wouldn't die up on Zynon, but I could have gotten shot in the head. I trusted my home wouldn't stab me in the back and would help me, and that definitely backfired. So why was I trusting Krisian?

It was probably because I believed in the good of people. I believed everyone was capable of kindness and compassion, and it was only society that turns people evil. If one could separate themselves from a toxic society and the beliefs that surrounded them, they would be kind and helpful to those in need. At least that was what I hoped and strived for.

But as for the man who was helping me through the crowd right then, I didn't know what to think. He had a point saying he could have easily turned me over to the guards. There was no reason to be doing this even if he was delivering me to Byron. The guards also wanted to turn me in to Byron, so he had to have been telling me the truth—he wanted to help.

Which begs the question of why? It was a known fact that he hadn't liked me when we were kids. He used to come over, tell my mother we were the best of friends, seem all cheery and whatnot, and then pick on me for hours and do whatever he wanted. He wasn't the worst person I was around growing up, but he certainly didn't care about me. Did something change? Or perhaps he wanted something from me. I would naturally give it to him since he was indeed saving my life, but I still wasn't sure if that was his true motive or not.

And how did he know it was me under this veil? And that I wasn't the one who killed my mother? My heart felt as if it were being squeezed. My dear mother was gone—taken away from me by Byron. She was the person I loved most in this world.

My poor sister witnessed it all at such a young age. She shouldn't have had to see that—Byron should have made sure she was in her room or something. If I had waited for my mother to speak later, would she have been all right? Or would Byron have sent that assassin at the same time? No matter the case, it just wasn't fair. She shouldn't have had go through that. It was all my fault.

I shouldn't have come here. My mother was dead because of me.

I tried to push back the thoughts—knowing that it wasn't my fault. I shouldn't have to fear coming home because of some other person. No, I needed to remember that this was all Byron's doing and none of the blame was on me.

Was this what Cor and Zach felt like? Such shame and humiliation? That they were used in such a way that led to the death of another? I didn't want to feel like this—I wanted it all to go away.

But I knew it wouldn't. Not until I made Byron pay.

I had never felt such hatred and disdain for someone until that moment. I thought I had hated him for how he treated me and for hurting Cor, but nothing compared to what I was feeling at that instant. I now understood firsthand what Cor must have been feeling, along with Ellie and Zach. And they lost everyone they ever cared for.

We rounded a corner to head to the stairwell that led up to the level my room was on. Krisian clearly remembered where it was as he was a couple of steps ahead of me. I kept my eyes out for guards, but they all seemed to have been at the front, helping people evacuate.

We climbed up the stairs, and my legs instantly were screaming at me. Krisian didn't seem to have much trouble, however, as he was used to all the buildings around here, not to mention he probably got to swim and build his strength up in the water. I had not gone swimming in the two years I was on Mu as I didn't want Cor to find out the truth of who I was.

We heard steps coming from above us, and Krisian and I quickly hid around the corner on the closest floor. As the guard came down the stairs, I aimed my gun full of tranks at him and fired. The guard fell over and rolled down the stairs. I felt a bit bad as he was probably injured from the fall, but he had also sided with my uncle, so the guilt was minimal.

Krisian and I listened carefully, and it didn't seem as if there were any other guards coming down. We ventured back up and eventually made it to the level my room was on.

We carefully made our way down the halls, searching for guards. None were posted, and it didn't seem the two that Cor had knocked out, tied up, and placed in a closet earlier had escaped yet. That was lucky for us as they probably were out for vengeance.

Making it to my room, we quickly closed and locked the door behind us. I took a big breath of relief.

"Okay, so, what's going on? Who was that person you were with?" Krisian asked as he took a seat on my couch.

I gave him a look. "What's going on? How about you tell me why you risked your life to help me?"

He looked away. "I... Look, after you left and everyone forgot about you, I realized how corrupt our society is. I began to feel bad for things I had done to you. I mean, we were kids, but that doesn't make it right. I know that many people in our zone hate you, but there was no reason for that. Even with how I treated you, you were always nice to me. I guess that just really stuck and I decided to be a better person. When I saw you, I thought I could return the favor and help. I couldn't just stand by and watch an innocent man be killed, and I wanted to make sure the princess got away safely. I have a child of my own now. She's only a year old, and I couldn't imagine anything happening to her."

He seemed genuine. Perhaps I had trusted the right person after all.

"I guess it doesn't matter if I tell you the truth or not, as I'm a wanted man anyway. As my mother was saying before… everything, I just got back from Zynon where the shooting took place."

"Where the Silurians shot everyone?" he asked.

I shook my head. "No. Well, it was them, but they had been tricked. Byron was behind it—he forced a Kausian to disguise as their leader, like tonight, and ordered them to shoot everyone. They could have resisted, yes, but it was still Byron behind the attack. It was also Byron behind the attack on Kaus a few years back. He was the one who'd gotten the codes and gave them to the Silurians. Then tonight it was Byron who found a Kausian to disguise himself as me and kill my mother."

Krisian leaned forward, setting his elbows on his legs, processing the information I had given him. "Why would Byron do all this? He's always stood by us Sirians and our way of life. He's like an uncle to all of us."

"Because he wants to destroy all the other nations. He wants the humans to rule and for there to be no half-bloods like me." I shrugged. "But how this is going to help him achieve that, I don't know."

Before Krisian could respond, there was a tap on the door. I pulled out my gun and waited. It was faint, but it was the knock code that Cor and I had established for situations like this. I quickly went over and opened the door. There stood Ellie and Zach. Cor was on Zach's back, looking worse than I had ever seen him before.

"Cor, what happened?"

# CHAPTER XXXI

Cor

I knew I was a wreck, but I didn't like how Gabe was looking at me. It was with such surprise and sorrow and pity. It was the worst feeling for me to be pitied.

Granted, I didn't like how Ellie was the one who'd carried me to safety either. I was supposed to be the one protecting her, not the other way around. But now I was weak and was making them all worry. I hated it.

Zach and Ellie helped me over to the couch and sat me next to the Sirian who had helped Gabe.

"Byron had a Kausian prisoner and let him take his frustrations out on me. I'm fine. I'll just need a minute or so," I explained. "Zach filled us in on what happened. I just don't understand Byron's intent. Do you have any idea?"

Gabe shook his head. "No, I don't."

"I think I might have an idea," the Sirian next to me commented.

I turned my attention to him. "Right, and who are you?"

Gabe answered, "This is Krisian. He was… a friend from my childhood. He helped me get up here, and now we're figuring out what to do and why Byron would have done… what he did."

I squeezed his hand. I wanted to say I couldn't believe Byron killed his own brother's wife, but that wasn't true. I could most definitely believe that.

"I think what Byron is trying to do is to get Sirians to hate half humans and other species in general. If he truly wants humans to take over, what better way to deal with Sirians than to make them retreat back underwater? Many people here don't think we should ever leave the Sirian Zone, so it's not a far stretch. It also doesn't help he's been backing people here in their belief of keeping their culture excluded from the rest of Mu."

That didn't seem that far-fetched. If he didn't have to fight the Sirians and could simply get them to leave, then he wouldn't have to worry about them. What better way to do that than to make it seem like a half human wanted the destruction of their kind?

Which was why he had the Kausian appear like Gabe—someone Byron had made everyone despise since he was born. Byron had been working on this for years. What was he truly capable of?

Gabe shook his head. "That… that's not possible, is it? I mean, people don't hate what I am so much that they would all stay here forever, do they?"

Krisian shrugged. "I mean, most people don't care either way. They just don't want you ruling. Once the princess was born, they never really thought about you again. But now, with it appearing as if you killed your own mother, I think they would shut everyone out. I'm not sure what will happen in the next few weeks. It's possible they'll put out a notice for all Sirians to return to this city. That's what the Silurians did, although for a different reason entirely. While there are some things we need to trade, that's still possible without completely opening up. It's what we did in the past."

If I remembered my history correctly—history that Byron had taught me when he was training me—the Sirians used to live on the beaches until they figured out how to make a city underwater. Once they'd left the land behind, they stayed underwater for generations, only coming up to trade. It wasn't until four generations ago they'd come back to living on the land. Once humans and Lyrans began advancing in technology and culture, so to speak, that was when they decided to start intermixing and learning from each other. And that was when relationships started to form and commingling began.

Which then brought us to Byron's grandfather wanting to destroy all the other nations.

"I think it is going to be impossible to turn anyone against Byron," I commented. "There's really no use. He's thought of everything."

No one else responded as they knew I was correct. I pinched the bridge of my nose.

"What we need to focus on now is how to get out of here. Anyone come up with a plan?" I asked.

Krisian nodded. "I have an idea, but I'm not sure if it will work." He took a deep breath, then nodded to the glass. "You all can escape through the glass."

# CHAPTER XXXII

Ellie

I wasn't sure if he was joking or not until Gabe nodded.

"I was thinking the same thing. The only way out of here is if we hit the emergency exit button and seal off this room to open the glass to the outside."

It made sense that all the rooms that faced the ocean had that feature. It was like any building on land—break the glass and jump out and hope for the best. The only problem was, it wasn't as if we could break back into the city. No, we would have to swim all the way to shore, where they would probably chase us most of the way.

Oh, this was so not going to go well.

Gabe continued as he scratched the back of his head. "Truth be told, I didn't want to suggest it because then all my stuff will be destroyed in the process. But seeing as I probably won't be welcomed back ever again, I guess it doesn't matter."

I definitely knew that feeling. I had lost all my belongings when our home was destroyed. At least my life was saved, but sometimes I can't help but think about the photos of my family, some of the trinkets given to me by my brothers, my favorite stuffed toy.

This was a bit different, however, as Gabe would be shunned from his home for no real reason. Byron had made it appear as if he had killed his mother. Even if we could somehow prove that wasn't him, it might have been too late for him to be accepted. They already didn't like him, and now they believe he had taken their queen's—his own mother's—life. It must have been the worse pain imaginable.

And he seemed to be keeping himself together quite well. I had a feeling all the anguish would come rushing to him once his brain had time to settle down. That's how it had been for me. There was a time of shock before it actually hit. That shock was probably the strangest, emptiest feeling in the entire world.

"What about Cor?" Zach asked. "How is he going to swim if he can't even stand? Not to mention he has many open wounds."

I glanced at Cor in his state. It was true—he was bruised and weak and bleeding still. Swimming as far as we needed to was not going to be easy. We weren't exactly close to any coast, and it was going to take a lot of strength to swim miles.

"Leave me behind—I'll find my own way out of here," Cor said.

I couldn't believe what he was saying. As if after everything we had been through, then finally back together, we would break apart again. I shook my head. "No, we aren't leaving you behind, not after what is going on."

"I can't swim, Ellie. Unless you have some kind of plan, then I suggest you leave me here and I'll find a way to escape. It's not as if I haven't gotten myself out of worse scrapes."

Zach nodded. "Cor's right. There's no way he's going to be able to swim with those injuries, not to mention the water might get them infected."

Although I knew Zach was saying that because he was genuinely concerned, I didn't like he was playing with the idea of leaving a friend behind. Was it because he actually didn't think we could make it? Or was he still mad at Cor?

I frowned. "What if we wrap them really well? There has to be waterproof bandages in your bathroom, right, Gabe? Then Gabe and I can tie something to Cor and help him along."

"I do have waterproof bandages. And I agree with Ellie. There's no way I'm going to leave you behind, Cor. We're all in this together. I can't imagine my life without you if something were to happen."

Cor shook his head. "You two are idiots. There are going to be people after us. They are probably currently out there circling the palace, making sure we don't pull this stunt. There's no way we can fight them and swim away with me in this condition."

I knew he had a point, but there would be no way he would be able to hide until he was strong enough to fight and run on his own. He had to escape with us. It was his only option. We could make this work. I bit my lip, trying to think of a way we could get him out of there and not make him a liability.

"How about you hold the gun and we pull you? Like if you were on the back of my horse while I steer. Then all you would have to do is shoot people and cover our backs, and Gabe and I can swim as fast as possible. Can you do that?"

Cor frowned, as if pondering on that idea. "I can. But I still don't think you'll be able to get away that quickly. It would be better if I stayed here."

"No. You aren't staying here, so just suck it up and help us come up with a plan." I turned to Gabe. "Do you have any spears or underwater weapons we can equip ourselves with?"

Gabe got up and started going through the closet. "Although I never learned how to use these weapons, as I never had the need, all rooms are equipped with some just in case we're invaded."

He pulled out some automatic harpoons, underwater rifles, and knives and placed them on the ground. I stood above them and nodded.

"Good. This will work."

"Ellie…," Cor began.

I pointed my finger at him. "Quiet, you! I didn't carry you down over a half dozen flights of stairs for you to stay behind. No, you are coming with us whether you like it or not."

He frowned but didn't resist. I picked up the rope. "Okay, we'll tie it around your waist and the ends around Gabe's and my waist. Zach, you are strongest and always were the fastest at swimming, so you should be in charge of having weapons and battling if need be. Gabe and I can focus on swimming, and Cor can focus on shooting and keeping the guards at bay. Sound good?"

"I can also help Zach," Krisian said.

Gabe shook his head. "No, I can't let you risk that. You have a family to get back to."

"You are very outnumbered and need help getting to the mainland. Once we're all there, I can simply head back as I doubt they'll recognize me. I'm not someone popular, and in the water it's hard to see anyone's face."

Gabe seemed as if he were going to argue some more, then shrugged. "If you want to help, I won't stop you. But it's going to be dangerous."

Krisian patted Gabe's shoulder. "I know."

We started to put everything together. I tightened the rope around Cor, Gabe, and me.

"This is going to work, right?" I asked.

Gabe nodded. "It has to. Now, are you all ready?"

Cor, Zach, and I all transformed into Sirians and nodded.

"All right, here goes nothing." Gabe flipped open a panel and clicked a few buttons. Everything then proceeded to shake.

# CHAPTER XXXIII

Zach

This was soooo not going to work.

There was a loud alarm echoing through the room as a large metal wall rolled down from the ceiling in front of the door to the hallway. The lights then flickered off as the glass only slightly lowered, letting in a rush of water.

Whoever engineered it to open was rather clever as it only opened a tiny sliver at the top as water poured in at a not-so-alarming rate. As the water level rose, all the contents of Gabe's room began to float. As the water touched our skin, all our skin began to shift into a slimier substance and our feet turned into finlike shapes so we could swim easier. Although not quite the same as when we Kausians shape-shifted, the Sirians were the closest species to us when it came to somewhat changing form.

The water kept spilling into the room and slowly engulfed us all. We were careful not to get hit by any of the objects and furniture that filled Gabe's room. Once the water reached about five feet, the glass receded the rest of the way and the room filled up in an instant.

It was strange being underwater and not having to worry about breathing for a while. They couldn't stay underwater for really long periods of time, but we could stay like this for at least a few hours, of which we would be able to make it to the surface and get some air. But that didn't mean that my lungs felt like this was possible. The absence of breathing was strange.

The moment we swam out of the building, there were guards headed straight for us. There was at least a dozen or so, and they didn't look like they were going to try to capture us for questioning. No, they were going to aim to kill.

Gabe was the one to lead us, and Ellie quickly followed. Cor was faced toward the guards, his weapon at the ready. They weren't quite close enough to shoot, so we focused on swimming and preparing ourselves.

I had my weapon ready as well and swam behind Ellie. Gabe's friend Krisian was on the side with Gabe. I glanced back to find that the guards were gaining on us. Soon they would be able to shoot at us, and we had to be ready to try to dodge, which was not going to be easy while swimming.

I really wished we'd spent more time actually attending swimming lessons.

Gabe seemed to know where he was going, which was good. I could barely tell which way was up or down. We kept pushing forward, but it was no use—the guards were much faster.

If we didn't have to focus pulling Cor, I believed we could have been quick enough to get away from them all. I didn't want to leave him behind either, but Cor was good at escaping things—I doubted he would have been caught. Then again, he couldn't exactly just walk out of town once his leg was better. No, he would have had to go through some kind of exit, and he would have been spotted even if he were using his powers. Not to mention who knew how long it would have taken for him to heal. There would have been no way for us to come get him if need be. The Sirians would probably be closing their gates soon.

Cor tried his best to kick his leg, but I saw the grimace on his face. Even though we could transform into different species, that didn't mean we could heal up wounds instantly. We did heal at a faster rate than other species, but not quick enough in this case.

The guards were getting closer and closer, and I turned to face them. I had never fought someone underwater, and I didn't particularly want to at the moment. But beggars couldn't be choosers, and I was just happy we were still alive. How long that was going to last, however, one couldn't say.

I aimed my underwater rifle at them and fired.

# CHAPTER XXXIV

Gabe

What were we going to do? There was no way we were going to escape the guards. We either had to kill them all or create a distraction.

But what sort of distraction would we be able to pull off at this rate? We were already in the water without any sort of gear other than weapons. What could we even do? It wasn't as if we could hide in the open sea like this either. We were literally fish in a barrel for those guards.

Zach was the first one to shoot, and surprisingly enough he managed to hit one of the guards. That still left almost a dozen after us. I kept on swimming with Ellie, pulling Cor behind us. It was the only thing we could do since we didn't have any long-range weapons. I swam as fast as I could, and Ellie was able to keep up with me, but Cor was giving us drag and the guards were gaining on us.

This was not good.

Cor began to fire his own weapon at the guards. He apparently was either just very used to firing a gun or he had done a fight underwater before as his first shot hit one of the guards. Either way, I was impressed.

The next few shots, however, missed. The guards swam closer, and I felt a bullet graze my arm. Red began to color the water around me.

Shit. Double shit. Triple shit.

There was no way we were going to make it out of this alive. We were outnumbered—outgunned—and it was taking everything I had to keep swimming. We needed something, anything, to distract them. But we had nothing.

Krisian shot a few times at the guards and then swam up to me. "I'm going to create a diversion. I need you to keep on swimming and not look back or come for me."

What was he suggesting? Was he going to sacrifice himself? I shook my head. "You can't be serious. They'll kill you! I'm not letting you sacrifice yourself for this fight. It doesn't have anything to do with you."

"But it does—it has to do with our people. I have to do this, or there will be no way you can escape. We aren't making it out of here alive if we continue."

Before I could counter, he began to swim toward the guards.

"No! Don't!" I called out, but it was too late. I watched as he made his way straight to the guards. Zach stopped for a moment, staring, then realized what he was doing. Zach turned to me and swam.

"We have to move quickly! Or what he's doing will be for nothing."

I knew he was right, but I wanted to stop and help him. He had sacrificed everything for me, and I felt I didn't deserve it.

Krisian began shooting in a frenzy, taking a couple of the guards out in the process. Two of the guards were able to make it past and pursued us. Cor aimed his gun and fired, taking both of them down.

I let out a breath of relief, but it wasn't over yet.

Krisian was still alive, and perhaps he would make it out of there unscathed. Perhaps he would be able to take out all the guards on his own.

Krisian was dodging and swimming in such a melodious way that it almost appeared like a dance as bullets and harpoons went by him. I watched as he shot down guard after guard until only a couple were left.

We were making distance now—perhaps we would get out of this all right. Perhaps we could do it.

There was one guard left. Krisian could do it—I believed in him. He and the guard struggled as Krisian tried to get the guard's weapon from him. He must have been out of bullets.

And that is when it happened—the guard's spear went right through his chest.

"No!" I screamed. I knew I had to keep pressing on, but I wanted to stop and cry. I wanted to cry for everyone I had lost that day. I wanted my mother back —I wanted my friend back.

His wife would wonder why he never came home. His daughter would grow up without a father. This wasn't fair—none of it was fair. I felt tears form in my eyes only to mix with the salt water that filled the ocean.

I had to live another day, just for them.

I kept pressing farther, swimming away from my home, knowing it was possible that I would never be able to return.

# CHAPTER XXXV

Cor

Gabe's friend had sacrificed himself for us.

I couldn't believe what I had seen. That Sirian was willing to give his life so that his prince could live.

So perhaps there were more Sirians like him. Perhaps they all didn't hate half humans and other species like Byron thought. Or perhaps that friend was the only person who would stand tall and fight.

The only problem was it was all my fault. I was a liability—I had caused us to slow down. If I hadn't gotten caught by Byron, none of this would have happened. I would have been able to help everyone instead of slowing them down.

I could never make this up to Gabe. His mother and friend were dead. Everyone in Kaus was dead. I only brought chaos. I didn't deserve these people who wouldn't leave me behind.

The question was, would I have done the same in their place?

Would I have left Gabe behind? Or Ellie? Or Zach? Or would I have risked my life to save them? I honestly wasn't sure of the answer. I wanted to say I would help them no matter what it took, but a voice deep in my heart said that I wouldn't have. It said I was selfish and would do anything I could to save my own skin.

And for some reason I felt that the little voice was right.

Knowing the truth made it hurt even worse. I had caused the death of so many people, and yet people keep helping me. Why was that? Why did they think I needed their help?

Why did they think I deserved their help?

We were too far gone for the remaining guard to try to swim after us, not to mention we outnumbered him now. He was more than likely going to swim back and report what had happened. They would send men after us, but at least we could get away for the time being.

I turned to face forward and tried to swim a bit on my own so Gabe and Ellie didn't have to use all their strength to pull me. It hurt though, as my leg was aching as much as it had when I first woke up—if not more. It would take days to heal, if that even. I wished we Kausians could heal quickly like we could transform, but that wasn't the case.

It was a good two hours before we saw the shoreline. We surfaced to the top and took a breath of the salty air. It felt good to breathe again, as it was always so awkward to be underwater for that long of time even if we didn't have to breathe.

Ellie, Zach, and I transformed back into Kausians, just in case someone was on the beach and spotted us. We couldn't be too careful and didn't want to be shot on the spot for transforming. We slowly made our way across the water to the closest piece of land, which was a wooden dock of the Human Zone capital. This area had many ships prepping to go fish or trade with the Pleiadians and go down to the Sirian Zone. We, of course, stayed clear of any Sirian ships—just in case.

We pulled ourselves on the solid ground and lay on the dock for a moment, gathering our breath and strength. The sun was starting to go down in the distance, which meant we had gotten back right in time for dinner.

Zach was the first to stand up. "Well, I don't know about you all, but I need some food, some drink, and a place to sleep for a thousand years."

Gabe lifted himself up. "I agree. All I want right now is a bed and some booze. Food would be nice as well."

Ellie and Gabe helped me up, and I had my arm around Gabe as we headed toward the closest tavern that had places to sleep. I didn't care if we all had to share one bed or not. I could have crashed on the floor at that point.

We stepped in a small establishment, still dripping wet. Everyone glanced our way for a minute, then paid us no mind. I let out a breath I had been holding.

Stumbling to the bar, we all sat down. Ellie put her head on the bar as I waved to the barkeep, who was a human man who appeared to be in his seventies with silver hair and a curly mustache.

"Can we get a few beers over here?" I asked.

"Make that a whiskey," Ellie mumbled, but I wasn't